THERE WAS A KNOCK AT THE DOOR...

Modern folk tales for troubling times?

This book is the result of a project conceived by the people behind the *New Weather Institute*, and *Bread, Print & Roses*. Decades of campaigning for a better world still finds us all in troubling times. So the book brings together writers, poets, economists, climate change experts, activists and artists. Each works daily in different ways to make the world safe from systemic threats, but has become aware of the limits of simply throwing facts at people and hoping for change.

Instead, they've decided to take a new approach, and to try and tell some better stories. They are very modern, yet rooted in ancient story telling traditions. We hope they open doors...

There was a knock at the door...

23 modern folk tales for troubling times

Edited by Andrew Simms

Foreword by Philip Pullman

THE REAL PRESS/New Weather Institute
www.therealpress.co.uk/www.newweather.org

Published in 2016 by the Real Press with the New
Weather Institute.
www.therealpress.co.uk
Introduction is © New Weather CIC, while all rights
to other contributions are all held by the individual
authors.

ISBN (print) 978-0992691998

Contents

Cover illustration by Annes Stevens.

"We sense new weather
We are on our marks
We are all in this together"

Carol Ann Duffy

Foreword

Stories are one of the most ancient and most effective ways of making sense of the world. There are some very stern people who think that stories can't be important or useful because they're only 'made up'. How wrong that is!

The human imagination is profoundly important, and when it turns to exploring the problems we human beings find when we try to live a good life in a world we seem to be simultaneously destroying, there is nothing more valuable or worth encouraging.

I'm very glad to see these stories and I hope they find the audience they deserve.

Philip Pullman
2016

Introduction

Andrew Simms

"Tell me a story," my daughter said, in the cottage, on the island, in the middle of the sea. The day was fading; a lighthouse began to turn, brushing the bedroom curtains with its imploring beam. I didn't know what to say. There were facts about the world and its problems I could endlessly relate, a desolate mountain of information that no child would want on their horizon. But, a story? I wasn't sure I knew any. I would have to make one up, but something that could hold a child's attention?

Suddenly calling on creative thought made my mind ache, like demanding immediate action from an unused muscle. Yet, in my life as a campaigner, I was always trying to tell a story of the possibility of a better world. Too often, clearly, I bypassed imagination. As we only know the world through the stories we tell, this was a great failing.

After decades of effort to find equilibrium with our life-supporting ecosystems, and to reverse inequality, humanity is hurtling toward the cliff edge of catastrophic, irreversible climate change, powered by a divisive, winner-take-all economy, high on fossil fuels. In the chaos and anxiety that ensue, anyone easily identified as 'other', such as migrants and refugees, become politically exploited as scapegoats, made out to be the causes of our insecurity, when they, too, are victims of a system-wide failure. All these issues and more can be found in the landscapes of these tales.

The importance of the environmental movement needing to tell better stories became the focus of a long conversation I had with the author, Philip Pullman, for a chapter in a book called *Do Good Lives Have to Cost the Earth?* During the conversation, he revealed for the first time a link between the damage done to the fabric of space and time by the 'subtle knife' (in the trilogy *His Dark Materials*), used to pass between worlds, and the climate damaging tracers from aircraft he gazed at in the sky above his Oxfordshire home. That is some of the background to this new collection of modern folk tales. It is meant as storytelling for its intrinsic, creative satisfaction, as a way of understanding and coming to terms with the world, and as a way compellingly to reimagine it.

Mythology is the cultural soil in which folk tales

grow. Cautionary stories about human over-reach, for example, get continually reinvented in the tragic events of Icarus and Daedalus. Such a story is so compelling, writes Karen Armstrong in *A Short History of Myth,* because it expresses, 'a universal desire for transcendence and liberation from the constraints of the human condition.' Fly too close to the sun, like Icarus, and you will fall. Enjoy flight within the tolerances of the wood, wax and feathers keeping you aloft, like Daedalus, and you can still safely soar. Here is an ancient myth that couldn't fit better for a civilisation wishing to flourish within planetary, climate boundaries. Mythology, says Armstrong, gives us 'the discourse we need in extremity'.

Folk stories have often emerged as ways for people to reconcile and assimilate the extremes of experience. In Europe during conflicts such the 30 years' war in seventeenth century Central Europe, related famines and other periods of great hardship, they have allowed people to come to terms with the darkness that privation can reveal. Abandonment, abuse, death and cannibalism are frequent visitors in early versions (often later sanitised) of many folk and fairy tales, from Hansel and Gretel, to Little Red Riding Hood and Cinderella.

Writers like Philip Pullman and Angela Carter

have done much to reinvigorate this tradition. Like dreams they allow us to organise, face and move beyond things that we struggle to come to terms with, and which can seem incomprehensible. Bruno Bettelheim envisioned the fairytale as a place where children could explore issues such as death, abandonment, loss, fear, witches and monsters, and create their own interpretations which would enable them to better understand and cope with 'real' difficult or traumatic experiences in their lives. In *The Uses of Enchantment*, Austrian child psychologist Bettelheim wrote about how fairy tales, in particular, were places where children could explore the darkest happenings on the journey through life, primal fears, witches and monsters. This, he suggested, allows children then to create their own interpretations which enable them better to understand and cope with real, difficult or traumatic experiences.

As the iconoclastic Victorian critic of both art and economics, John Ruskin, said of landscape painting in a way that still has wider resonance: "All great and beautiful work has come of first gazing without shrinking into the darkness."

We can all tell stories. Some of the people in this volume are writers by trade, but others come from the front lines of several vital, pressing contemporary issues. These range from climate activists to financial analysts, champions of local economic revival and a campaigner for more humane drugs policy. All of the stories appear for the first time in this volume, with just the exception of the winning from a writing competition on mainland Europe (A Little More Space), and the poem by Carol Ann Duffy.

A key point of this book was to invite people who daily argue with facts and rational argument to try, against immense odds, to improve the world, to set loose their imaginations and experiment with other ways of telling their story. It is one small gesture to encourage a culture of telling better tales, because if we can't find better stories than the ones which keep the world locked on a path of mutual economic and environmental self-destruction hope will flee.

Some of the stories we tell ourselves in the face of these challenges can be less than helpful. Public figures, like the businessman and advocate of aviation expansion, Richard Branson, and the physicist Stephen Hawking, say we must look out into the galaxy to find other homes for the future of humanity. In late 2015 the discovery of the nearest Earth like planet was announced, circling a star system called Wolf 1061.

Wolf 1061b is described as 'quite likely a larger

and hotter version of Venus.' Venus, remember, suffered a version of runaway global warming. Wolf 1061c however could be like a mini Neptune, or it might be rocky and habitable. Cue acres of media coverage and wild, romantic speculation that, not only might there be life 'out there', but also that there might be somewhere else for us to go in the Galaxy if we make too much of a mess of our oddly habitable home planet.

There is a problem though. At 14 light years away – doesn't sound much – using Deep Space 1 technology it would take you 267,452 years to get to Wolf 1061c – or just under 9000 human generations. And, imagine your disappointment if, when you got there, it turned out to be like Magaluf on Friday night. But wait, in late 2016, another Earth like planet was found – Proxima Centauri B – and this one is much closer at only 4 light years away, or just about 76,000 years to get to. It also has no days to speak of in the conventional sense, locked in a kind of geostationary orbit, is scorched by its sun on one side, in deep frozen darkness on the other and is subject to deadly solar flares.

Escape from Earth is both an awfully romantic notion, and a trap that sets humanity up to fail, as it somehow also lets us lose our grip on the need to preserve life here, where we know it already exists. If they found on Mars a single blade of grass, there would be ecstasy at ground control and blanket media coverage, while all the time we trample the abundance and diversity of life on the ground beneath our feet. The secret is that we are the life we seek 'out there', and we are right here already. Stories of wonder and intrigue may just remind us of that fact.

I noted some time ago in another book I wrote called *Cancel the Apocalypse* that: 'Perhaps the greatest gift of space exploration remains that it enabled us to see ourselves as an island planet, where the greatest wonder is to be found around us, between us and even within ourselves. In Milan Kundera's *The Book of Laughter and Forgetting* there is a scene involving Kundera and his father who, recently having suffered a stroke, has difficulty speaking.

The father had, for years, been studying and writing about Beethoven's sonatas and their magical variations. His barely coherent remarks trigger in Kundera an understanding that the greatest journey is not into the infinity of the external universe, but to 'that other infinity, into the infinite diversity of the interior world lying hidden in all things'.

In Britain during the Second World War, when conservation of resources was a matter of life and death, with fewer material goods to spend money on (paradoxically, the war effort meant a vibrant economy and high employment levels) people spent more on experiences, getting out, having a good time, going to dances, the theatre and movies. More culture, the telling of stories in many forms, filled the space of consumption.

As we move to world where it becomes necessary, more satisfying and desirable to substitute experience for passive, material consumerism, the telling of stories plays many roles. It fills a void, nourishes the soul and hones our ability to reimagine how we might live in the world.

Decades of environmental activism have rested on a belief that change is a rational process. Present the right facts, to the right people at the right time, and the right thing was supposed to happen. It didn't, and hasn't. Campaign after campaign brilliantly at exposed the mess the world was in, but very few ever told a compelling tale of how we all might thrive within planetary boundaries. In Proverbs, it famously says that 'where there is no vision, the people perish.' Yet, in a refrain now so common it is attributed to many different voices, it's said that it is easier to imagine the end of the world than a change to our economic system. Imagination, then, may just be the key to our survival.

It would be wildly deluded to think that any small collection of stories will lead to any particular, concrete change in the world. No, these are just to be enjoyed in their own right. But they are also an invitation to think differently about problems, to relax, experiment and exercise our collective imaginations.

It is a great paradox that while we all know that the present is, for many, positively very different from the past, we find it hugely difficult to believe that the future will be much better than the present. Such imaginings tend to be dominated either by dry, technological fantasies, or dystopias.

Not only might a popular culture of storytelling make us all feel better, more creative, engaged and connected, it could save us from the 'death by dry technocracy' that permeates politics and corporate working life. In exercising our imaginations more, we might find the world as it is leaves us less care worn. We may, too, find it easier to picture and believe in those changes we need to an economic system that drives inequality, crushes the spirit and corrodes our ecological life support.

On the second night in the cottage on the island in the middle of the sea, as the evening drew in, the lighthouse lurched awake to sweep the night, brushing the curtains in the bedroom where my daughter nestled down, prepared for sleep. "And, then what happened?" her voice demanded. "Of course," I replied. "There was a knock at the door..."

1

The magician's house

Jan Dean

When the magician came he made a promise.

"Work for me for a year and a day and at the end of your service I will give you your heart's desire. Whatever you ask for, I will give it."

Well, who could refuse? Genet couldn't. Genet didn't.

And suddenly, as if from nowhere, the magician produced a contract. The long scroll of thick yellow parchment crackled as he smoothed it open on the table.

Next a pen and inkpot popped out of the air and into Genet's hand. She wrote her name at the bottom of the scroll and the magician poured a puddle of hot wax onto it. Red wax. Wax as warm and wet as blood. Then he pressed his ring into its softness and smiled.

"There. Signed and sealed. Now everything is agreed."

So Genet worked for the magician. "I don't need much," the magician said. "Just get up early in the morning and light the fires for me. It's all I ask."

"How wonderful," thought Genet. "All I have to do is light the fires and my work is done. My life is sweet, my life is easy. I am the luckiest of women."

And so it seemed. For one week and a day all Genet did was light the fires – a big one in the kitchen and a small one in the magician's workroom. But then a strange thing happened. The magician's house grew. In the middle of the night, Genet woke and all around her the walls of the house creaked and groaned. The floors grumbled and roared. The roof screeched and howled. Then the great noise subsided and everything fell still again.

"I have been dreaming," Genet said and she drew the bedcovers up around her shoulders and slowly drifted back to sleep.

But Genet had not been dreaming. When morning came and she got up to light the fire she found that the magician's house was twice the size it had been the night before. Instead of an upstairs and a downstairs the house was now four storeys high. Instead of four small rooms on each floor there were eight medium-sized rooms on each floor. Instead of one fireplace in the kitchen and another in the workroom there were sixteen fires to light.

It took a long time to gather enough kindling for sixteen fires, and even longer to chop enough logs to burn. For two more weeks, Genet lit sixteen fires every day, and kept them going with fresh logs, and cleaned the ashes from the grates, and swept the hearths and kept them neat and tidy. While she worked Genet kept in mind the magician's promise. In less than a year she would have her heart's desire.

"I can do this," she said. "It is only lighting fires, after all. Not hard work. My life is sweet. My life is easy."

And so it was, but when two weeks and a day had passed, the magician's house grew again. The stones of the walls heaved and ground together like great granite teeth. The slates of the roof clattered and scraped. The wooden floorboards, the rafters and joists screamed like banshees. Oh, how the house howled as it grew and it grew. And oh, how Genet cowered in her bed as she heard it. For this time she knew she was not dreaming.

When silence fell she rose from her bed and, by the flickering light of a lantern, she walked through the magician's house. For hours she walked. Through all sixty four rooms, on all sixteen floors. As she walked she counted the fireplaces. Five hundred and twelve.

When morning came, she went to the magician.

"There are too many fires," she said. "I can't light them all."

But the magician was not sympathetic. He unrolled the long scroll with the blood red seal and pointed to her signature.

"You must," he said.

Then Genet turned and ran.She wanted to go back to her old home. She reached the magician's door and threw it open and gasped at what she saw. The magician's house was now so large that it had swallowed up the whole village. Where once whole rows of cottages had stood, now there was only the magician's house. A great bloated building as high as a hill. Genet wanted to go back home, but now she had no home to go to. And where were all the people of the village? They were gone too. Genet looked at the grey stone of the magician's house and shivered.

As the weeks passed the magician's house grew and grew until it was a monstrous mountain of a house. And Genet lived inside it, pale and thin as a stick, moving from room to room, from fireplace to fireplace, covered from head to foot in grey ash.

If she met the magician on her journey through the endless rooms she always said the same thing. "My life was sweet, my life was easy. When the world was the world and not this monstrous house. Give me back my world. Give me back my world." Then she would weep. But the magician simply said: "It is my world, now. You gave it to me. And you can never have it back."

So Genet tended the fires that burned and burned while the house grew and grew until it reached the coldest limits of the world. There the fierce flames and furnaces of the magician's house began to melt the ancient ice. But tears and melting ice were all one to the magician, Genet knew that now. She knew too that her world was gone and she could never have it back. The best she could hope for was to forget how lovely it had been. So when a year and a day had passed that is what she asked for.

"Magician," she said. "Give me the gift of forgetting."

The magician gave her a black velvet cloth.

"Put all those things you never want to think of here in this black cloth. Then fold it gently round them. Wrap them in the darkness. Bury them in night."

Quietly Genet took her memories of home and the good green world and folded them in forgetting. She buried all of them in the darkest corner of her mind where they would never bother her again.

"Now I will leave this house," she said.

But she could not. For now the house was all there was.

2

The Maw Maw bird

Andrew Simms

There was a scratching of taloned feet among dust and stones, then an odd knock at the door. It sounded like a clam batting away a crab's claw (now, I have never actually heard such a thing so, like you, I am imagining this is how it sounded).

Sat, lost in a book at the kitchen table, Florence Burntwood, a fearless child without brothers or sisters to hide behind, leapt up and ran to open the door. More cautious children might have peered first from the window to see what was there. Still others might have hidden in a cupboard until the peculiar noise went away, or asked somebody else to investigate. Not Florence. Curious and confident, she flung the door wide open.

"Maw," said the creature.

"Pardon," said Florence.

"Maw, Maw," it said, twice, to underline its point. A disconcerting rumble came from what she assumed to be its stomach.

"The creature must be hungry," thought Florence and went to the larder to fetch fresh, white bread and two slices of cured ham. Placing them on the wooden kitchen table she looked again at the animal stood in the doorway. It had short legs, with knobbly knees, ending in fat feet, from which twisty talons sprang. Though strange, it was unmistakably a bird of some sort. It had stubby feathers on stubby wings that were shaped like odd sized dinner plates. A bulbous beak like a Dodo's sat beneath very large enquiring eyes. And, it seemed to make only one sound.

"Maw," it said once more, hopping across the threshold, and skidding slightly on the kitchen floor tiles, before ruffling awkwardly up onto the chair in front of the food. Here it stopped, stared and ate nothing at all.

"Why won't it eat if it's hungry," wondered Florence. As she opened her mouth to say something, she thought she saw its already large eyes widen more, slightly, as if in anticipation, and its disorganized, rather dull feathers fluttered.

"I will call you the Maw Maw bird because that seems to be all you can say," she said. "You are strange, stranger than the chicken on our farm that was born with two heads. We called it Cluck Cluck. It ate twice as much corn as the other birds but laid no eggs because the two heads could never decide where to roost." Strange things happen on farms and even in her short life Florence had seen a few. Sometimes, though, it was hard to tell what she had seen with her eyes and what with her imagination.

But the Maw Maw bird appeared entranced and clacked its beak with approval. As it did so, Florence noticed two feathery flaps either side of its face. They hid ears that disappeared into its head like water wells into the ground. What looked like fungi grew deep inside. Florence felt nauseous.

"Flip," she said. "You're even odder than the piglet we had that was born with four ears. Its hearing was so good that when the truck from the slaughterhouse arrived in the farmyard, Lugs (that was its name, farms are much too busy places to spend time inventing fancy, clever names) was already ten fields away. He heard it coming."

Florence paused for a moment, dreamily, then continued. "I do believe Lugs got work with a piano tuner who was going deaf and feared for his livelihood. Together they did very well, tuning instruments over four counties. The last I knew, their success and growing reputation led to a contract as sound engineers in the biggest recording studio in the city. All the most famous musicians now queue for their services."

The Maw Maw bird burped contentedly, flopped from the table and waddled out of the door. Its twisty talons scratched the kitchen tiles as it went. Florence, puzzled, watched it go, the food still untouched on the table.

That night she dreamed of animals getting jumbled up: a rabbit with the head of a fish, a cow with giraffe's legs, and pigs with dog's tails and wings. But in the morning, when she ran to check the barns, all the animals still had their right parts in the right places.

The day passed uneventfully until Florence heard again the scratching and tapping of an odd, seemingly hungry bird. It interrupted as she was making a potion from washing-up liquid, oats, pepper, lemon, vinegar and blue ink.

"Maw, Maw," said the bird, with those wide expectant eyes as the door opened.

Florence went to the larder and, knowing the bird didn't like bread and ham, took out dried apricots, nuts and a slightly smelly cheese with blue bits like the patterns you see in marble (it was worth a try, after all, who knew what Maw Maw birds liked).

The food was ignored, but still the irregular looking creature sat at the table, hopefully. Today, it seemed slightly different. Its legs looked a little longer, the knees less knobbly, feet less fat and talons not so twisty. Were its feathers less ruffled too, and wings now a similar size? The beak seemed more banged-into-shape, like a piece of worked iron whose final appearance was not yet clear.

"You are an impossible puzzle," said Florence, "a mystery with the last chapter missing." It reminded her of something. "In our family and on this farm, I have found many things that are hard to understand. Once a tree branch fell on Uncle Roderick's head and later when he returned from drinking beer at the ale house, he was singing songs in Russian, a language he did not understand. Uncle Roderick spoke not a word of French, nor Spanish, Cantonese or Swahili. He could barely understand even the accent of city folk and generally preferred not to talk at all. But after being hit by a tree, he wouldn't stop talking, but only in Russian, so nobody knew what it was about."

The Maw Maw bird was transfixed as Florence warmed to the task of sharing her past.

"I think Uncle Roderick felt quite lonely being the only Russian speaker in the village. Then, one day a lonely bear wandered out of the woods, terrifying everyone. Until, Uncle Roderick passed by and said something to the bear. Nobody knew what, of course, but the bear took his hand in its paw and together they danced along the high street to the tune of some imaginary music."

It is hard to imagine eyes larger than those on the Maw Maw bird at that particular moment, which as we know were already very big, nor a burp of satisfaction louder than the one which followed the end of Florence's tale. "The last I heard," she said, "Uncle Roderick and the bear opened a dance school especially for animals and people, and toured the great theatres of Europe performing nightly to packed houses and wild applause (very wild in fact, as there were as many animals as people watching in the audience). The howls of the timber wolves were especially loud. I can tell you Maw Maw bird, all that was hard to understand, but it is not nearly as mysterious as you."

Just as the day before, when Florence stopped speaking, the food remained untouched on the table, and the odd bundle of features that refused to eat shuffled from the kitchen, only this time it was slightly less awkward as it went.

That night Florence dreamed of an exotic garden where all the plants wilted because there was no rain to nourish them. She woke determined to feed the Maw Maw bird if it returned, and spent the day collecting the most delicious food that she knew. In the garden she found ripe pears, plums and raspberries. They were sweet and tasted more interesting than apples and strawberries, which were good but a little predictable. For extra flavours she collected mint and fennel whose feathery leaves she loved, as soft to the touch as cashmere, and they released a sweet scent of liquorice and honey.

In the larder, she found a paste made from crushed olives, and savoury biscuits with little seeds that came from poppy flowers. She cut a cucumber into triangular wedges for crunchiness and boiled pasta for chewiness. Melting butter and sugar in a heavy old iron saucepan, she stirred in some oats to make her favourite flapjack. And as it sat cooling she waited, pleased with her work, and utterly convinced that no living creature, including the Maw Maw bird, could resist the best food her world had to offer.

Shadows stretched across the garden. She thought it would not come. Then... tap, tap, tap.

An altogether different looking bird stood before the open door. Taller, thinner, much thinner, gaunt even, Florence thought, and very awkward. The Maw Maw bird moved as if each leg and wing was not quite sure what the other was doing. Its feathers had grown long. They pointed in every direction at the same time, and were now the gaudiest collection of colours you have ever seen. The Maw Maw bird looked like it had crash-landed in a paint factory. Its talons were now stubs at the end of long disorganized feet. The beak was long too, pointed and, well, beaky. But the bird was unperturbed by its new appearance and gyrated happily toward the table, where it sat in front of the sumptuous plates of Florence's carefully prepared delights, and ate... nothing.

Instead, it looked at Florence, again expectantly. After her effort preparing the food, it would be fair to say that Florence was exasperated. She was actually a lot more cross than that, but to use the right word to describe her mood would be impolite. She felt rejected, worried for her peculiar new visitor, and helpless, all at the same time.

"You were odd already, but now not eating has made you completely weird," Florence said to the mixed bag of birdiness that looked into her eyes unwaveringly, not missing a single word.

"Maw Maw bird, you cannot live on nothing. A mouse may live off only crumbs, and tiny ants feed off even tinier aphids on the flowers in our garden. But everything that lives must eat. You have eaten nothing, even though I have given you the best foods that I know. And now you are in a terrible state and I am afraid that you will die, and it will be my fault because I could not find anything that you can eat. Yet you return to my kitchen door each day and – in spite of your peculiar appearance – you do not seem sad or distressed." Florence paused and turned her gaze inwards. She climbed around inside her memories to see if there was anything useful. Then she remembered.

"One day, I found an abandoned baby blackbird too young to fly, and thought that it may die. I kept it in a box in a room where the cat couldn't go, dripped milk into its mouth and fed it stale bread. Slowly it grew stronger and stronger. In a week it learned to copy the sound of our grandfather clock, and caused terrible confusion. Mother and Father got up in the middle of the night when the blackbird sounded the hour of breakfast, then they fell asleep at tea time when they thought they heard the chimes of midnight.

"When it became a healthy grown-up bird, I set it free and he stayed around the village creating more chaos. People would fall asleep on their bicycles if they heard the wrong chime or take evening baths at lunch time. One night, a group of very drunk men on their way home were fooled into thinking it was time to go to work. Of course, they all lost their jobs. They were found the next day asleep at work and smelling of booze. They were so confused that they fled from their angry families to the land of the midnight sun. There, it was always daytime so they wouldn't make the same mistake again (no, they would make different ones).

"Another time, I found a lost child. She'd drunk a cup of nettle tea at a country fair which turned her hair green. Her parents no longer recognized their daughter and went home without her thinking she'd run away. The poor thing was shunned. Grown-ups wouldn't help her. They don't like children with green hair, worrying it might be contagious. Instead, she came home with me. I gave her brown tea which turned her hair back to a normal colour. She stayed and played with me for the rest of the year."

"Maw, Maw," cried the Maw Maw bird.

Florence thought for a moment and continued: "It turned out she was like a chameleon. When we picked strawberries her hair turned red, and blue when it was time for blueberries. In autumn, as the leaves on the trees changed colour, so did her hair. You'll be pleased to know that when the leaves fell, her hair stayed put. At Christmas, she became as white as the snow and in spring bright green like the fresh shoots sprouting everywhere. But when it was time for the summer fair again, we were careful to return her hair to its proper colour and she found her parents by the same toffee apple stall where they had blankly abandoned her the year before. Now, they were overjoyed. I also gave her a special potion to slip into her parent's tea. It would make them see only in black and white, just in case their child's hair changed colour again and they would not recognize and reject her."

"So, you see," sighed Florence, "I am good at helping all sorts of creatures and people, but I cannot help you, the strangest sort of all, and that makes me very sad."

Yet the ragged Maw Maw bird didn't look sad at all, quite the opposite. It looked rather pleased with itself. If you have ever heard a frisky stag bellow at the top of its voice, you will know what it sounded like when the Maw Maw bird burped again. Flumping off, it left behind a very bewildered little girl.

After scoffing all her favourite food – Florence didn't believe in waste – she fell into a deep sleep and dreamed of animals with no manners, ones who changed shape and colour, and never explained themselves.

The next day there was no tap at the door. Or the next, or the next, or the day after that.

Sunday came and there was neither school nor chores so Florence went for a walk in the woods.

Carried on a lilting breeze came the sweetest, unfamiliar voice. "More, Florence, More," it said. She looked around, and then up. That singing voice again, like a harp played slowly: "Tell me another story."

But Florence was, for once, speechless. Sat in the tree was the Maw Maw bird, but it was not the Maw Maw bird, and yet it was. She knew by the smiling expectant eyes. Everything else about it though was different. Elegant, sleek and perfectly proportioned, its feathers were still different colours but they were like the tiles of a beautiful mosaic, and formed themselves into pictures of fantastic landscapes and animals that changed as it spoke. And, it spoke. Not only had it never eaten, Florence realized, until now it had never before spoken a word other than a raucous 'Maw'. She was now entranced.

"Thank you, child," said the Maw Maw bird. "If you had not fed me, I would never have grown into my full self."

"But you ate nothing," Florence replied. "I offered you bread and ham, and made you my best dishes but you didn't touch a single one."

"That is because it is not food that I eat," explained the vision in the tree, "but words. And, the better the stories that they are put in, the more nutritious they become to me. Because your stories were so good I have become the best I have been for many ages. Because you have called me the Maw Maw bird, I am now the Maw Maw bird, that too is part of your story. But, in days gone by, I have been called many other things. There is only ever one of me. Each time I hatch, I must find a child who loves words and stories. If they are patient with me, and talk to me, I turn into this. If I fail, within the turn of four seasons, that wonky bird you knew as me days ago must crawl back underground for one hundred years, before I can emerge again.

"But now I am my full self and unique to you, I will live as long as you do. We will tell each other stories and travel this and other worlds in our minds. Often we will go on very long, real walks too. At the end of our story I will become an egg again."

All the time that the Maw Maw bird spoke, Florence saw flashing pictures first form and then dissolve in the bird's feathers. She saw mountains and sand dunes, great rivers and laughing crowds of people. She already knew the world through books and her imagination, but Florence had never seen many of these things. Now she knew that any story she could imagine she would be able to see as if real in the feathers of the Maw Maw bird. For a moment, neither bird nor child said anything. But a look and an understanding passed between them.

It might not always be easy, they knew, but this life was going to be amazing. "More," they said to each other. "Let's tell more stories."

- the end (of the beginning)...

3

A little more space

Fien Veldman

The first meeting of the Parliament of Things had opened. Everyone seemed slightly uncomfortable under the weight of their newfound autonomy. At the same time, there was a brittle sense of revolution in the air.

The Horizon was quiet. Ever since the Things acquired a right to speak for themselves, he had suppressed the urge to do so. Am I even a Thing, he wondered? What I look like and where I am has always been decided by somebody else. Most of the other Things were firm. Substantial. He, on the other hand, always felt unsteady.

Behind the pulpit was Bronze. Bronze glistened while he presented the many ways in which he was used by people. Of him, weapons were made; statues, church bells. There was even an entire age named after him. Iron and Stone nodded approvingly. While Bronze chronicled his own importance, The Horizon gathered the courage to make his way up to the podium. He needed to contribute – it was his Parliament too.

While he proceeded to the stage, everyone watched. Even Bronze quietened down. The Horizon had never been this aware of his extensive proportions. He was boundless, limitless, and he felt rather dizzy.

Bronze had stepped aside. The Horizon cleared his throat.

"Hello, everyone," he said, unsure whether this was the appropriate way of addressing the Parliament.

"Thank you for your attention." His nervousness faded slowly.

"Man has always thought of us as instrumental. Things and Technologies to be used, Animals and Plants to be eaten. Me, the Horizon, to be painted, photographed, and appreciated – but always in the background." He decided to make a joke.

"So this position, of me being in front of you, is very new to me." His audience grinned.

"First of all, I would like to express my gratitude to all of you. Without you, I would be empty. You constitute the view that I am the basis of. You complete me." He wondered if he was being too sentimental, but decided it was acceptable. It was a meeting of great importance, after all.

"That being said, there is a problem I would like to address." He took a deep breath. "I am becoming too full. I feel myself almost overflowing with matter. It is too much."

He felt the eyes of his audience upon him.

"Not to be unappreciative or anything, of course not," he said, because in the back of his mind he wasn't entirely sure whether this shift of political power would last. "But humans are everywhere, and they are taking up quite some room." He looked up, into the audience. "What I mean to say is: I could use a little more space."

The Animals, the Plants, the Technologies and the Things considered it for a while. A little more space. Just a bit more room without human interference. Forests without tourists camping in them; skies without airplanes full of travellers cutting through them like knives; mountains that weren't being climbed by venturesome individuals. That's what they all needed. A little more space.

After a moment of silence, a thunderous applause resounded. The Horizon turned red. He felt slightly embarrassed by this mighty support, but proud at the same time. It was unanimously decided that the first rule of the Constitution would be as follows:

"Dear humans, we would like a little more space."

4

Mrs Midas

Carol Ann Duffy

It was late September. I'd just poured a glass of wine,
   begun
to unwind, while the vegetables cooked. The kitchen
filled with the smell of itself, relaxed, its steamy breath
gently blanching the windows. So I opened one,
then with my fingers wiped the other's glass like a brow.
He was standing under the pear tree snapping a twig.

Now the garden was long and the visibility poor, the way
the dark of the ground seems to drink the light of the sky,
but that twig in his hand was gold. And then he plucked
a pear from a branch. – we grew Fondante d'Automne –
and it sat in his palm, like a light bulb. On.
I thought to myself, Is he putting fairy lights in the tree?

He came into the house. The doorknobs gleamed.
He drew the blinds. You know the mind; I thought of
the Field of the Cloth of Gold and of Miss Macready.

He sat in that chair like a king on a burnished throne.
The look on his face was strange, wild, vain. I said,
What in the name of God is going on? He started to laugh.
I served up the meal. For starters, corn on the cob.
Within seconds he was spitting out the teeth of the rich.
He toyed with his spoon, then mine, then with the knives,
the forks.
He asked where was the wine. I poured with a shaking
hand,
a fragrant, bone-dry white from Italy, then watched
as he picked up the glass, goblet, golden chalice, drank.

It was then that I started to scream. He sank to his knees.
After we'd both calmed down, I finished the wine
on my own, hearing him out. I made him sit
on the other side of the room and keep his hands to
himself.
I locked the cat in the cellar. I moved the phone.
The toilet I didn't mind. I couldn't believe my ears:

how he'd had a wish. Look, we all have wishes; granted.
But who has wishes granted? Him. Do you know about
gold?
It feeds no one; aurum, soft, untarnishable; slakes
no thirst. He tried to light a cigarette; I gazed, entranced,
as the blue flame played on its luteous stem. At least,
I said, you'll be able to give up smoking for good.

Separate beds. in fact, I put a chair against my door,
near petrified. He was below, turning the spare room
into the tomb of Tutankhamen. You see, we were
        passionate then,
in those halcyon days; unwrapping each other, rapidly,
like presents, fast food. But now I feared his honeyed
        embrace,
the kiss that would turn my lips to a work of art.

And who, when it comes to the crunch, can live
with a heart of gold? That night, I dreamt I bore
his child, its perfect ore limbs, its little tongue
like a precious latch, its amber eyes
holding their pupils like flies. My dream milk
burned in my breasts. I woke to the streaming sun.

So he had to move out. We'd a caravan
in the wilds, in a glade of its own. I drove him up
under the cover of dark. He sat in the back.
And then I came home, the woman who married the fool
who wished for gold. At first, I visited, odd times,
parking the car a good way off, then walking.

You knew you were getting close. Golden trout
on the grass. One day, a hare hung from a larch,
a beautiful lemon mistake. And then his footprints,
glistening next to the river's path. He was thin,

delirious; hearing, he said, the music of Pan
from the woods. Listen. That was the last straw.

What gets me now is not the idiocy or greed
but lack of thought for me. Pure selfishness. I sold
the contents of the house and came down here.
I think of him in certain lights, dawn, late afternoon,
and once a bowl of apples stopped me dead. I miss
    most,
even now, his hands, his warm hands on my skin, his
    touch.

Carol Ann Duffy is a patron of the New Weather Institute.
This poem first appeared in her collection, *The World's
Wife* (Picador Classics).We gratefully acknowledge her
permission to include it here.

5
Rapunzel
Suki Ferguson

A knock came at the door. "What's this?" thought the woman. "Who knocks on my door so late, on such a wild night?" She'd heard the wind creaking the trees outside, and seen the rain battering her window panes, and had lit a fire to blot it out. And now a stranger was knocking.

She opened the door and peered beyond the cottage's light. A hooded and rain-draggled girl stood shivering, and she cried "Oh, let me in, please! I have a question for you, kind lady. No one else can answer it, and the villagers tell me you can help. Will you?"

The woman was mystified, but did not show it. She invited the girl in, dried her close-cropped hair, and sat her to warm before the fire. There, the girl told her tale.

"Ever since I can remember, I lived in a tall tower, with only my mother for company. The limit of my world was the circumference of the topmost chamber. Yet, when I looked from the window, I could see all the country around, full of trees and meadows and hills. Mother would sit with me to look sometimes, but mostly she stayed away. She never said where it was she went. I was glad when she left, lonely though I was.

"She could only reach me by climbing up to my window, up the trees and the wall, and later, my long hair, which I put round a hook so she could climb it like a rope. When I was small, she left me toys, and when I became a woman she left me needlework so I could make the pretty dresses she liked to see me wear. She gave these only when I was good, and though I dreaded her visits, her gifts filled my days.

"One day, I sat at the window in tears. Mother had left me again, and before she did so she had made me do the things I never liked to do. She was angry that I cried afterwards, and she'd always whisper that I was lucky, and should feel proud that she found me beautiful enough to protect from the world. I tried to feel glad of my looks and the long hair that so enchanted her, but I never was. So I looked beyond my chamber, and wept.

"That was the day things changed. As I looked down at the forest beyond, I saw a man standing amongst the trees. He was the first stranger I had seen in all my years, and he bewildered me – he looked so tall and strong, and free. He had seen me, and called: "What a pretty scene, my princess! Let me cheer your sad face. Let down your long hair!"

I longed for kind company, and learning that I was not as alone as I had thought thrilled me. He leapt up the tree, and I saw his good looks. I let down my hair. As he began to climb it, I grew afraid of his strangeness, but could not stop him from reaching me. How did he know the way to get in?

He answered that thought before I stammered it aloud. He reached me, vaulted into my room, and laughed to himself. "I knew that the old witch would not go to such troubles unless the morsel is a tasty one!" I knew then that I had made a mistake, and that he was not a friend to me. He treated me just as my mother did, and when he left I felt more desolate than ever before. His words about her troubled me. How had he known her ways? Was I known of elsewhere, and what sort of lives were led there? I decided I would leave this trap and find out for myself.

"So I began to break each of my long hairs off, at the root, and wind them into a rope. I tied it at the hook, and climbed down from my tower. That is how my long journey here began, and now I hope to have come to the end of it. The world has been frightening and I have no money, but I am glad to be free. But please: is it true that you know the answer to my question? Why have I not lived as others do?"

The woman had listened to the story in silence, and stared into the flames of the fire. Finally, she replied.

"Yes, I can answer your question. You lived that way because I chose it."

The girl started, but the woman turned and looked hard at her. Stay, she said, and listen to me.

"Twenty years ago, I was tricked by a lover and he left me in trouble. I was shunned and alone: I starved for food. I'd go thieving to feed myself, and in desperation I stole from a grand and terrible lady. When she caught me taking apples from her orchard, she gave me a choice: death, or giving up my child on the day of its birth. To save my life and that of my baby, I agreed to her bargain. She took you the day you were born, and paid me for my sins. I only heard of her ways later, when I visited the village and overheard gossips. They knew what I had done, and I remained an outcast. But they must be who sent you here today, and for that I'm grateful.

"Forgive me, child. I thought I did best by us both, but I never expected such a life for you. But you're here and safe now – stay with me – please. "

At this, the woman wept, and the girl reached out to hold her mother's hand. The answer to her question was a sad one, but she was glad to forgive it all the same. For her other hand rested on her swollen belly, and she understood that not all life is born blessed.

6

Merlin and the small dog

David Boyle

"It's no use," Jack's mum sighed as he came in with Timothy, their cocker spaniel. "The miners have moved onto the site. There's nothing we can do."

For six months now, Jack's mum had signed petitions and written letters to the prime minister, trying to stop the other side of their hill from being turned into a big open cast coal mine.

"They can't have done," said Jack, taking off his coat. Timothy looked around for his dinner

"They can and they have. There's nothing more to be done and, once they've dug up that side of the hill, they say they will dig up this side. We've done everything we can."

"Not our woods. They're ancient woods. Mr Murgatroyd said so."

"I'm afraid so, Jack," said his mum, looking tired and miserable. "We'll just have to move, though goodness knows where we can move to. What is that thing that Timothy's brought in?"

"Yuck," said Jack bending down. Timothy had dropped a muddy looking bone at his feet. He was wagging his tail and looking pleased with himself.

"Oh, throw it out into the garden will you?" said Jack's mum. "He's brought quite enough mud just on his paws."

Jack loved the woods that stretched up the hill behind the estate. He loved living under the ancient hill – Merlin's Hill it was called – and he had begun over the years to feel that they were his woods. At least his and Timothy's. It was Jack's job every morning and evening to take Timothy for a walk there, and he hardly ever saw anyone else walking there.

The thought of having to move away, while the miners demolished the old hill bit by bit, was just awful. He threw Timothy's muddy bone out of the back door and settled down to his own dinner, miserable about the future – not just because he was sad, but because he could see his mum was so sad as well.

"I have to leave early tomorrow morning," said his mum. "I'm on the early shift. Can you take Timothy for his walk and then put him in the kitchen? I'm so sorry Jack, but you'll have to give yourself breakfast this time."

It poured with rain in the night. Jack was woken by his mum letting herself quietly out of the house at dawn and lay there thinking about their hill.

Then he dozed and only just managed to wake himself in time. He pulled on his school uniform, grabbed some toast and put Timothy on his lead. He peered outside the back door and caught sight of the muddy bone which Timothy had found the night before. It had been washed by the rain.

Strange. Jack peered closer. This was no ordinary bone. It seemed to have holes in it. He picked it up and ran it under the tap. It looked extremely old, but there was no doubt about it. It was carved as a whistle.

"Look what you found, Timothy. You are a clever dog. I wonder who lost this." Timothy wagged his tail.

On an impulse, Jack put the whistle to his lips and blew. A faint note sounded. He tried again. Some old mud blew out of the end. Finally, he opened the back door wide and blew with all his might.

To his surprise, a long low note came out. It shook the leaves in the tree in the next door garden and seemed to echo in the air. Then he remembered the time. He locked the door, picked up Timothy's lead, put his homework by the front door, and set off for the woods.

"Come on Timothy. I haven't got long this morning. I've got to be in school in fifteen minutes."

Once they were through the gate into the woods, he let Timothy run and he streaked ahead up the hill. He could hear barking in the distance.

"The mining company must be starting already," he said to himself. "Timothy, come back! I have to go to school!"

Jack felt crosser and crosser as he ran uphill, along the slippery mud paths, after his dog. To his surprise, he found he still had Timothy's bone whistle. He blew it again furiously. At this rate, he was going to be very late. He looked behind him. He could no longer see the road or the estate.

At long last he could see Timothy ahead. As he got closer, Jack realised that he was not alone. Sitting on an old tree trunk, talking to Timothy, was an extremely old man with a very long white beard and a hat that made him look a little like Father Christmas. He appeared to be wearing a dirty leather dressing gown.

Jack was nervous of talking to people he didn't know and he stood and wondered what to say.

"Thank you for keeping my dog. I have to get to school," he said.

The old man turned to him crossly. He looked more wrinkled than anyone he had ever seen. "Who are you? Why have you called me?"

"I haven't called you," said Jack, feeling very confused.

"You called me. You called me twice. Nobody has called me for a very long time indeed. So tell me, has the dawn broken? Has the spring begun? Has history arrived again?" Jack stared at him.

"Don't stare, boy. You blew the whistle. You called me out of sleep. You did so twice."

"I'm sorry," said Jack pulling out the bone pipe. "Timothy brought me the whistle and I didn't know what it was. I can give it back. It isn't damaged or anything."

The old man held out his hand and took it. His hands were rough and bony and like the hands of an ancient badger.

"Nobody calls me by accident. You may not know the reason, but there is one. I know the world, boy. I may not have lived in it for a very long time, but I know its ways. What is your name?"

"Jack," said Jack trying to attract Timothy's attention. "I have to go to school."

"No doubt, no doubt. But there is a reason for this meeting. Nobody calls Merlin from out of the hill by mistake. Come with me, Jack. I will not keep you long. Follow me."

He rose as if he was a much younger man and, for

the first time, Jack could see that he was standing next to what looked like a great iron gate in the side of the hill. It was standing open.

He was just explaining that his mother had always warned him not to go anywhere with strangers, when Timothy leapt up, barked twice and headed through the gates.

"It seems as if your dog knows the way," said Merlin, his eyes twinkling. "You have blown the whistle. You must see what you must see."

Jack was horrified and beginning to be scared. "Timothy!" he shouted into the tunnel."Oh heavens..."

Merlin held the gate open. It creaked a little on his old hinges. Jack slipped inside calling for Timothy. Now he knew he was going to be late, but how could he leave his dog inside the old hill? He had no idea there was a gate. Why hadn't he seen it before?

The passage was very dark but straight, and it was lit by small glowing lamps.

"Glow worms," said Merlin. "Keep straight on until the very heart of the hill."

Their footsteps thumped on the hard mud floor. Occasionally a drip from the ceiling fell on Jack's head. In the distance, he could see an orange flicker which must have been from firelight. He felt himself shaking with fear. How stupid he was to have gone inside the hill. He might never get out again.

Finally, they were in a huge chamber. Jack could see a big fireplace with the flames gently licking around some logs. There was Timothy lying by the fire, looking a bit guilty.

"Timothy, you naughty dog. Come with me now, will you. Thank you, Mr Merlin, but could you help me us find our way out now?"

"A moment with you first, my boy," said the old man, beckoning him over, and for the first time Jack turned round and saw a sight that just made him gasp.

The cave was lit by burning torches along the walls. There seemed to be warriors asleep around the edge of the cave, all with long beards, glinting breastplates and swords beside them, covered in cloaks. They were dusty and some of them half covered in earth or by leather rugs. Behind them, Jack could see horses tethered in hay and weapons along the wall. Then opposite the fire, on the other side of the chamber, was a rough wooden chair and a man with a grey beard leaning heavily on the armrest. He also seemed to be fast asleep.

Jack pinched himself. The morning had been getting even odder, but he thought he must now be dreaming. Had he actually just stayed in bed? He desperately tried to wake himself up.

"Tell the king," said Merlin softly, indicating the sleeping greybeard. Jack could see a crown hung on the back of the throne. It was battered and needed a polish. The king himself was wreathed around with cobwebs. "Tell the king why you called me and then you may go, and you may take with you anything you see."

Merlin pointed next to the king, and Jack saw piles of plates of gold and silver, great jewels and broaches and chests of money, like a pirate's treasure trove.

How could he tell him, Jack wondered to himself? He looked fast asleep.

But Timothy thought otherwise. He went up to the throne and sniffed loudly. Then he growled and let out a great bark.

"Timothy, no!" shouted Jack, dashing over and finally putting the dog on his lead, tugging him desperately away.

But it was too late. The sleeping king moved. His eyelids flickered. He looked about him blindly.

"Is it day?" he asked in a rough voice.

"No, sire, but this young man has brought us news from up above. Tell him, boy."

Then Jack had a brainwave. Of course he had news and anyone living in this hill would want to know it. "It's true, your majesty," he said, unsure how to address sleeping kings. "It is true. The men have come with machines and they are going to dig up the hill for coal."

Slowly the king became more alert, sitting up straight in his throne. Merlin got nearer as Jack told the story of the petitions and the plans by the miners and the big company which had bought their hill. He talked about global warming and fossil fuels. Still, the ancient king listened.

"It is true what he says, sire. Our hill is in danger."

"You have done well, young man," said the king. "I salute you and I reward you. Take from the table anything you can carry. Take it before my warriors awake. Take it with my blessing."

"Thank you, my lord," said Jack. "Come on Timothy."

He walked over to the table heaving with gold, seeing it through piles of cobwebs and dirt. At the front of the table was a short sword in a beautiful jewelled scabbard. He lifted it up, blew off the dust and began to pull it out of its sheath.

But as he did so, a low sound echoed around the chamber like the shaking in the air he heard when he first blew the whistle. A wind began to swirl among them, and the cobwebs began to blow away.

"Not the sword," shouted Merlin from the throne.

"Not yet!"

Jack turned round to see the nearest warrior getting slowly to his feet, brushing the cobwebs away and blinking around him in the candlelight.

"Is it day?" he asked.

"No, no..." said Jack desperately, shutting the sword back into its ancient sheath and dropping it. "Go back to sleep."

All around him, the warriors seemed to be waking. He panicked, pulled Timothy close to him and ran from the room back down the passageway he had come from. As he ran, a voice echoed around him in whispers.

"Jack, Jack, Jack," it said. "If you had just drawn the sword and heard the horn, you would have been the happiest that was ever born."

Jack's feet echoed on the hard earth floor. Timothy's paws pattered next to him as they raced for the light in the distance.

There was the gate. Jack leapt through, scratching himself on the brambles growing round the entrance, which he hadn't seen before. Then he breathed a sigh of relief, raced down the hill as fast as he could go on the slope without letting go of the lead. Trees and bushes flashed by. Sometimes he skidded in the mud. He could hear his panting breath and only then remembered school. He was going to be at least half an hour late. He would have to explain to his teacher or he would be in trouble.

It took him ten minutes to get home, put Timothy in the kitchen with some food, and to change his muddy trousers and be back on the road to school with his homework under his arm.

The school gates were deserted. He had to ring the bell. His footsteps echoed through an empty school hall as he made his way to his classroom. As he walked, he tried to understand what had happened that morning, and tried to think of an excuse for being late.

The classroom door swung open.

"You're late, Jack," said his teacher.

"Yes, Mr Murgatroyd, I'm afraid I..."

"Yes, out with it? Do you have a note from your mother?"

"No, I..." The whole class was looking at him. He could see Neil and Robin giggling with each other. They were enjoying it.

"Jack, be so good as to inform us why you are late and then we can get on with what we were doing."

Jack stared at him.

"We're waiting," said Mr Murgatroyd.

There really was nothing for it. "Well, the truth is

that something odd happened to me on my way to school and my dog ran away down a hole in the hill..."

"Your dog," said Mr Murgatroyd, blinking a little...

"Yes, and inside the hill was a sleeping king, surrounded by sleeping warriors and swords and shields and gold and he asked me if it was daytime, and I told him about the new coal mine, and then – well, I got scared, and a ran out and I had to change my trousers."

"Your trousers?"

"Yes."

There was half a minute's silence and then the class erupted. The laughter lasted so long that Jack even began to laugh himself.

Mr Murgatroyd looked more and more cross.

"You will go and see the head teacher and do so now," he said. "I will not be made a fool of in my own classroom. Sleeping kings and warriors. I ask you. Now go!"

"But really, Mr Murgatroyd. It's true. It really happened."

"Go. Get out of my sight.

Neil and Robin were waiting for him at break time.

"You are an idiot, Jack. Where did you get that story from?"

As he walked past people from his class, they giggled at him. Within minutes the whole school seemed to know. There were jeers and pointing fingers. Jack hid himself away in the corner of the playground. Perhaps he wouldn't have believed the story himself. If only Timothy could talk, he would be able to tell people – but of course he couldn't. Perhaps it really had been some kind of dream.

It wasn't until they were back in the classroom, and Mr Murgatroyd had started on a lesson about France when he heard that familiar rumble – part horn, part shaking – that he had heard inside the cave. Nobody else seemed to have heard it. But a few minutes later there was the sound like horses hooves in the road outside.

"Please, Mr Murgatroyd," said Jasmine urgently from beside the classroom window that overlooked the road. "There is something going on outside."

"Ignore it please, Jasmine."

The noise got louder, as if horses were racing past the school gates. More and more, they could only think about the noise from outside. Finally, Mr Murgatroyd walked over to the window. Then he stood still and stared.

"I don't believe it," he said. "Class, stay seated."

But it was too late. Everyone in the class was crowding round the window and staring. Jack could hardly see past them.

"What is it? What is it?" said those children who could not push their way through.

Then the head teacher was at the door. "Mr Murgatroyd, there seems to be some kind of disturbance outside. I don't quite understand it. There are some people dressed as warriors riding down the street, and looking – I must say – extremely realistic."

"I can see. I can see," he said. "Jack, come here a moment."

Jack pushed through the crowd of silent children. There were his warriors, mounted on warhorses, galloping between the parked cars in School Road, with armed with swords and daggers. Streamers fluttered from the end of their spears. Their beards swept along in the wind. The tails of their horses swished in the air and their leather shields were clipped behind them. Then came the horns again. The air shook.

"Is that what you saw?"

"Yes," said Jack. "That was what I saw."

"Then I believe I owe you an apology. Any idea what they are doing here?"

Suddenly Jack did know. It came to him in a flash

as he looked up towards the hill.

"I think they are heading to the mining site."

Mr Murgatroyd followed his gaze. They were indeed heading around the other side of the hill. And in a minute or two later they were out of sight.

There was silence for a few moments after they had gone. Jack noticed his classmates avoiding his eyes. There seemed nothing to say. Nobody mentioned it at lunchtime. It was as if the sight of warriors charging down their familiar street had been too odd to talk about.

The head teacher gave the class a short talk about how some things are too strange to talk about outside the school. "I hope you all understand," he said. They did seem to a few moments later, Mr Murgatroyd was back talking about France as if nothing had happened.

It was certainly very strange. Nobody mentioned the warriors to Jack again. They seemed to be embarrassed about it, as if they had all been dreaming and didn't want to say so. But later that day, the mining contractor's trucks and diggers began to drive away from the site.

"How extraordinary," said Jack's mum a week later, reading from the newspaper. "Listen to this.

'International Fossil Fuels PLC, who had been granted permission for their super-open cast coal mine, have now abandoned the site. They blame geological difficulties.'"

"Does that mean they're going?"

"It does. We won after all. Our old hill is saved."

""Does that mean we can go on living here?" asked Jack.

"Yes, darling," said his mum. "Incidentally, you never told me how you got so muddy in your school trousers last week. I just found them behind the washing basket. They were covered in thorns and cobwebs as well. I don't know how you managed it."

Jack thought about his warriors often. Many times, he came close to telling his mum about them, but he never did – but he did wonder about all that gold. Sometimes, taking Timothy for a walk, he would try to follow the path he had taken that morning, looking behind every bush and bramble for the rusty iron gate that he had walked through.

He could never find it.

7

Horst and Gertrude

Hamish Fyfe

During a dark and freezing night, when the windows howled and the doors squeaked, a young mother was woken from her sleep by the crying of her children.

She knew the cry of her own children and could tell it from those of the windows and doors and from the cries of Hansel and Gretel, whose father, a good man, she had married recently. Moving quickly through the little, dark and noisy house, she found Horst and Gertrude and comforted them as best she could. The children's eyes looked wide and blue and questioningly right into their mother's soul.

"Momma we are hungry," cried little Horst as Gertrude snuggled up against her mother for warmth. So thin, so ill, thought her mother: what will become of us all?

Gently, she sang to the two little ones who lay painfully in her lap:

Erdő szélén házikó,
Ablakában nagyapó*.
Lám egy nyuszi ott robog,
Az ajtaján bekopog.
Kérlek, segíts én rajtam!
A vadász a nyomomban.
Gyere nyuszi, sose félj!
Megleszünk mi kettecskén.

Which, translated into English, means:

In a cabin, in a wood,
A little man by the window stood,
Saw a rabbit hopping by
Knocking at his door.
'Help me! Help me! Help me!" he cried,
"Wicked hunter shoot me dead."
"Little rabbit come inside,
"Safely to abide."

When the morning came, the mother, who was stepmother to Hansel and Gretel, made a terrible decision, one she had been dreading but knew she had to make soon. Stirring the thin porridge she so lovingly restricted in quantity, so that everyone in the house could eat, she could see that before long there would be no food and she would be able to feed no one. That terrible thought simmered in her mind as the last of the porridge simmered on the wood stove.

Seeking to speak to her husband where the children could not overhear them, she took him outside in the early dawn to a small grove of trees beside the house.

"Last night, the children cried and I could not help them. Husband, I cannot bear to see them like this and fear that all our children will die if the famine continues to mock our efforts to stay alive. Horst and Gertrude are the younger and the weaker ones, whilst Hansel and Gretel have wit and courage beyond their years. My poor dear husband, it is time for Hansel and Gretel to take their chances in the world beyond our care, unfairly plucked from childhood as they might be. Year after year, the crop has failed, the land is parched and the weather is cruelly changed. If they stay we will all surely die."

"Wife," said Hansel and Gretel's father. "When I married you, I wanted to take care of you and your children as I did for my own. I love you all and would not see harm come to any of you."

The man and his wife fell as silent as the windy sky and then the man wept. His wife walked slowly back to the house and her husband stood there for a long time before moving, as the last shadows of the night slowly retreated around him. When he finally stirred, the sun was flashing through the treetops in the wood so soft and beautiful that, had he not been so fearful, he would have been filled with happiness.

Returning to the house, the father looked at Hansel and Gretel, smiled, and said: "My two little ones, a great adventure awaits you in which you can show how brave and clever you are. Our mother has prepared a package for each of you to take with you on your journey." Then, with a heavy heart, he led the children out into the wood.

The rest you know...

8

Rowan

Sarah Woods

Nature wraps itself around the stack of rotting windows in the garden of the house, with bindweed and brambles. The rubble from the extension rattles with spiders and woodlice and snails. There's a crow's nest in the conifer at the bottom of the garden, and froglets grow their front legs in the pond by the old shed, under which a vixen has gone to earth, venturing out with her four cubs as dusk descends.

Inside the house, there's a cry. More animal than human, more howl than scream.

Something flies out from a first floor window and falls to the patio. An aqua knitted cardigan with daisy buttons. A yellow babygro with chicks on it. A white towelling babygro embroidered with a teddy bear. A pastel pink fleece blanket.

The new bi-fold doors bang open with too much

force and she's out. A woman, driven and directionless. Wracked. Lurching with an emptiness that fills the growing night. She takes a step further into the garden and the three boy fox cubs skitter away, falling over each other to get back under the old shed. Only the girl cub remains.

The woman scans the garden, looking but seeing nothing. Tortured even by the season, by its mothers and its babies.

"So many beating hearts," she says, almost aloud. "Even in this garden. Why, when all the world is moving, was my baby so still?"

The fox cub lifts her nose high. Smells the smell of blood. Of milk. And something dark like wet earth. Something gone. And the vixen watches her daughter from the corner of the old shed. Waiting for her to turn for home.

In bed the next morning, the woman senses the sound of her breath outside her body as she wakes. The room she's in. Him sleeping next to her, his right hand on her left hip. And something else - a baby crying. Sitting up, her breasts rush and fill, wet discs spread on her pyjama top. She can hear a baby crying, but it is not her baby. Yesterday crashes in as though through a ceiling too thin to hold it up. She bleeds. A baby is crying but it is not her baby. She bleeds still. And milk comes still. And her baby. She does not have her baby.

Out in the garden again, dripping milk and blood, the woman sees its hands first – reaching out of the long grass in front of the old shed. Just a few weeks old. Every mother runs through her mind and every child born as she picks the baby up. Its back dewy, its head warm, tucked into the crook of her right arm beneath a crown of soft, red hair, looking at her with grey-flecked eyes that say:

"Take me.
I am yours".

She takes the baby girl inside. Puts her to one solid, aching breast. Then the other. And they sleep, curled in the chair she had bought to sit in to feed her child.

JULY

This morning, and every morning as the light comes up, the woman is woken by the sound of Rowan gurgling in her cot in her bedroom next door. This morning, as she takes her in her arms, she notices a patch of dirt on her pillow. Earth. She pops Rowan in her baby seat, strips the cot and remakes it. Clean.

They sing: "Row, row, row your boat," holding hands, rocking together, each seeing themselves in the other's eyes. Rowan's grey-flecked eyes almost amber now, her red hair thickening by the day with a soft, bright, downy ripple running from her neck to the bottom of her back. She's already trying to turn over and soon she'll start to crawl.

In the garden, a cardinal spider runs from its web as the man shovels rubble into a barrow. Froglets throw themselves at the fence and at the fence again as the pond is filled in and bark chips cover the grass. They're getting the garden ready for her – a sandpit, swing, security lights to keep away trespassers. This will be Rowan's space.

Every evening as the light fades, the woman puts Rowan into her cot and they do not hear a peep out of her until first light.

"You're so lucky she's such a good sleeper".

"She's a good girl."

"Where does she get all her red hair from?"

"And those eyes."

The only thing that ever wakes the woman and the man is the foxes going through their bins.

SEPTEMBER

The barbeque has moved into the house. As the bi-fold doors are pulled shut, birds dip down for the corners of buns while a brown rat makes off under the flowering currant with half a chicken skewer.

A perfect summer evening fades and the woman puts Rowan in her baby seat in the sitting room. It's getting late.

"It's past Rowan's bedtime."

"I should put Rowan to bed."

"Rowan's usually in bed by now."

She says it over and over as dusk gives way to dark. When the guests leave, the woman and the man go to the front door to say their goodbyes. For a few moments, Rowan is alone. She looks out into the garden. So dark. The security light snaps on and there, on the patio, is the vixen, waiting. Rowan feels it in her coccyx first, then somewhere between her eyes and ears. She knows what will happen. Teeth now. Fur next. She kicks out from the baby chair with her strong hind legs and lopes to the sitting room door – too late. The woman and the man arrive in a chaos of sound.

"Where's Rowan!"

"It can't have -"

"Where is she, then?"

"Get it out!"

Rowan pulls herself back, into the corner of the room. She can see the garden. The old shed. But can't get to it. Rowan runs to the woman. As she crosses the carpet, the man raises the baby chair up over his head.

Out in the garden, the vixen waits by the corner of the old shed. The security light clicks on as something is thrown from the house. It skitters across the patio. The vixen walks to her child. Sniffs her open amber eyes. Sniffs her open mouth. Her fur, running from one end of her spine to the other, so red. Stands so still so long over her child that the security light clicks off. A movement in the bushes snaps it on and she is caught there. She looks up. On the other side of the bi-fold doors, another mother looks out.

9

Syrenka

Kirsten Irving

If the royal family had anyone to thank for saving them from a PR nightmare, it was the housekeeper, Mrs Gorse. Hooped but nippy, like an agitated bird, she dashed around the halls each morning, managing the greeters hired seasonally by the household. One of the Dutch girls didn't like her, but she'd be back off to university by the end of August, taking her scowl with her.

None of them understood the importance of the role here anyway - they whinged about the pay and ranted about having to put their bags through security every day without a thought for the welfare of their employers. What good was it to speak three languages if you were surly in all of them?

Nothing escaped Mrs Gorse's gaze. She had weeded out the odd thief, the frequent shirkers and the rule-breakers over the years without a thought. When your job was to oversee a shifting tide of recruits from all corners of the continent, you had to have a kestrel's eye.

That eye fell almost immediately on Karolina. A pretty girl from Warsaw, Karolina did not carp about the palace metal detectors, and didn't once complain about the minimum wage pay.

From the off, she worked hard, greeting everyone – even the brash Houstonites who wondered aloud where the nearest McDonalds was – with a warm and genuine desire to help. There was something odd about her.

It was as though she had been born for the job. Arriving fifteen minutes early each day to put on her uniform (unlike the others, who seemed to think nothing of arriving at nine in the morning in jeans and a Metallica T-shirt, clutching an un-ironed mass of fabric with the royal crest on it), she would wave hello to the gardener's assistant and make a quick cup of black tea with sugar, before taking her place in whatever location she'd been assigned that day.

The girl's amiable nature began to concern Mrs Gorse, just as a perfectly clean kitchen bothers a health inspector. At least, with the others, you could tell what they were thinking. Take the Dane, Klaus. He was usually wondering if his favourite serving lady would be working in the great hall that day, so he could get an extra-large portion at lunch. Or the

French girl, Annette, who was always smoothing her hair in case Ben from the grounds staff came by. Mrs Gorse could deal with people if she disliked or worshipped them. Anything in between was a source of great anxiety to her. She felt an overwhelming need to find some dirt on the neat little Pole.

It was a month into Karolina's employment when Mrs Gorse spotted her opening. The eldest son of the queen had returned home from university and immediately the summer staff became even more distracted than usual. A rower at Cambridge, Prince Richard was a well-built, horsishly affable young man. Not handsome, but sandy and likeable, and relaxed in a way that only the immovably rich can be. When the student noticed Karolina, he was clearly smitten.

Karolina, for her part, became suddenly shy, her Warsaw accent washing over her excellent English whenever the prince addressed her. When Richard asked her if she would join him for lunch, she became all but mute, and managed to convey that she was busy. Clearly, thought Mrs Gorse, she's starstruck. Obviously foreigners had always dreamt of meeting such important people. Explained why so many of them showed up here, year on year.

Eventually, the girl agreed to spend half her lunch hour with the prince, and they headed out together into the sculpted gardens. That was the first day Karolina was late returning to work, her apologies gushing forth over a barely squashed smile.

A fortnight passed and Karolina began to undertake tours, beaming throughout, and was always thanked profusely for her enthusiasm. They weren't to know that the heir to the throne was meeting their guide daily now, and had begun to joke about the future. While Karolina was blossoming with confidence, the prince had become somewhat nervous, as he hovered by the inner palace gates each evening after her shift, waiting for a goodbye kiss.

As soon as she realised how rapidly the pair were growing closer, Mrs Gorse felt a low hum of panic in her gut. She looked upon Richard as a son, having summoned his mother's convoy to the hospital when she gave birth to him. She had seen his first steps, and noted to herself his royal bearing, even as a tot. The idea of letting an unknown quantity like Karolina so close to him began to make her extremely nervous.

All I need is one thing, one fault to reassure me, she thought. I need to know she's not an assassin or a spy. Got to find the minor typing error in the manuscript. Now the thought had crossed her mind, that Karolina might be a spy, Mrs Gorse could not help imagining her vaulting the gates at night in a cat suit with a dagger, pushing open the door to a sleeping royal. But no, that was silly. Why do that when you could walk right in through the front door, arm in arm with the heir? When you could lay beside him and slip something into his night water, then kiss him goodnight and blame it on the housekeeper.

It's amazing what a royal seal and a threat of culpability can do for diplomatic relations. Hitherto embargoed international documents began to warm Mrs Gorse's hands. By desk light, she sifted translations of confidential government papers, hunting desperately for Karolina Nowakova. Too many, too many. Then she moved onto the gruelling task of searching the most common name in the Polish electoral rolls. Pulling up Karolina's HR record, Mrs Gorse cross-checked and cross-checked over several evenings, nearly giving up before checking one last ream of medical records. Jackpot.

Born Janek Nowak, the son of a dentist from Katowice. Son. Those arms around the prince of her country. My god, the bullet Mrs Gorse had just shot from the air. She printed out the records and ran wheezily through the staff quarters into the family wing, her unfit frame rocking like a ship, desperate for someone to see what she had found.

Karolina Nowakova's employment was terminated by the palace the following day. Failure to fully disclose identification records was cited, and the dismissed girl was asked to change out of her uniform, leaving it by the laundry before being escorted off the premises.

A few months later, the news broke that Prince Richard had gotten engaged to a girl from his college and photographs of her foamed from the covers of every magazine, alongside descriptions of how refreshingly normal she was in all the chaos.

"What was it like?" asked a pink-maned Ukrainian drag queen, as Karolina served up a weak tequila sunrise. "Working at the palace?"

"I do love to live through others," said a 6'5" Shirley Bassey nearby.

"I don't remember what it was like then," said Karolina. "Just how it feels now. Like every step I've ever taken has been across knives."

"Polish saying," she apologised, and began to wash a glass.

10

The Ogre

Andrew Simms

Endless war laid waste to the once great kingdom. Maya took control when her parents died, inevitable civilian casualties of an airstrike that they were told was against insurgents. Their house was destroyed and the neighbourhood levelled, so she gathered her younger brothers and sisters and decided to leave for Europe.

Fixers who she knew by reputation could arrange the journey, and hoped to pay with the few family valuables rescued from the rubble of their home. One, nicknamed the 'Ogre', was feared but thought effective. She led her siblings through the shattered city to the almost-abandoned suburbs where she thought the Ogre lived.

In the middle of flattened, burned-out and bullet-scarred buildings was one that seemed almost new – untouched or rebuilt she couldn't tell.

Maya expected the Ogre to be tattooed, sweaty

and hung with heavy jewellery. And, he was huge, but not like that at all. In the doorway, flanked by men with guns, stood a sharp, clean suit and a permanent, slight sneer. He would help but she, her brothers and her sisters, would have to stay overnight. A frown crossed Maya's face, but he said they would be safe, and could share a large, dormitory-like room with his own children.

A big, powerful-looking four-wheel-drive car, almost the size of a truck and covered in mud and dust was parked among several other, spotless and expensive executive limousines. The Ogre called this his Seven League Boots. Specially adapted with a suped-up engine it could outrun the police and check-point guards and, using its spacious boot, he smuggled people across the border. They would leave the next day before dawn, he said.

The Ogre took all Maya's valuables, even the precious pendant given by her mother on her eighteenth birthday that she tried to keep. He told her to make sure that she, and each brother and sister, took a blue blanket to sleep under from a pile that looked stolen from a UN aid convoy.

They were sent to where the Ogre's children slept while the Ogre went to another room with his cronies. But Maya, suspicious, followed and listened at the door. "When they are all asleep," the Ogre said to his cronies, "go to the room and use your clubs on all the children under blue blankets. They have no hope outside this country, we will be doing them a favour. And, anyway, I am too busy to take them across the border."

Maya saw that the Ogre's children all had finely woven blankets of soft, colourful yarn and suddenly she thought how they might escape. Slipping a pebble beneath herself so that it would be too uncomfortable to slumber she waited for the Ogre's children and all her brothers and sisters to fall asleep. Then, swiftly, she switched the coloured and blue blankets taking care to cover everyone's faces to hide their identities.

Later, when the cronies crept into the dimly lit room, unknowingly, with sickening thuds they bludgeoned to death the Ogre's children. As soon as they left, she quietly woke her siblings, took the keys for the Seven League Boots (she guessed they were the ones with the big boot on the keyring and a number '7' scratched into it), and sped from the suburb towards the border at almost unbelievable speed, easily outpacing the cronies who raced after her once they realized their mistake.

At the checkpoint, she explained what had happened and was taken to a large building that had air conditioning, smelled clean and was full of smart men and women working on computers. In the biggest office she was sat in front of man behind a large desk who seemed to be in charge. 'Reginald X. King', said the nameplate in front of him. Maya asked for asylum as she knew you were supposed to. King explained that the man who had tried to trick and kill her was known to him and had things they wanted. "I can arrange for your sisters to have safe passage to the European country of your choice," said King, "if you will do something for me."

Maya agreed, of course. She had no choice. "The Ogre has a list of routes and ports he uses to smuggle people, guns and drugs," said King. "We need that list." Maya took the 7 League Boots and returned to the Ogre's stronghold with incredible speed, arriving before dawn to hear him screaming at his cronies for their failure. While he was distracted, she crept into a room with filing cabinets, found a draw full of maps and directions, grabbed them and sped back to the border before she was seen.

"If I knew you'd find it that easy, I would have asked you to do more," said King, smiling, before adding after the briefest pause: "If you return and find me the list of all his accomplices, I will arrange for your brothers to have safe passage to the European country of your choice."

Maya felt tricked again, but still had no choice so

leapt once more into the 7 League Boots and went back to the Ogre's. This time, at the door, she could hear him weeping loudly and uncontrollably at the back of the house. But she could afford no sympathy. The terrified cronies had made themselves scarce and Maya found more files with lists of names and contact numbers and fled.

"What a resourceful young woman you are," said King. "I have one last task for you. If you do this, I will arrange safe passage for yourself to the European country of your choice. But there is one condition: you must tell no one what I ask you to do."

What King wanted was details of the Ogre's bank accounts, their location, numbers and passwords. Knowing something was wrong, but with no option, Maya agreed. But she asked for all the documents for her, and her brothers and sisters to be prepared so that she could take them on her return.

Back at the Ogre's, everything seemed deserted so, confident, Maya went straight to where he kept his information. This time, though, with a roar the Ogre leapt from behind the door and grabbed her.

In a rage, he was about to squeeze the life from Maya. Thinking quickly, she said: "Ogre, do not kill me. I can take you to the man called King who plots your downfall."

The Ogre paused so Maya hurried on: "He made

me steal your information for the foreign powers to save my brothers and sisters, and now he wants all your money and I think he wants it for himself. He is well protected but if you let me live, I can bring him out to you because he does not suspect me."

The sneer returned to the Ogre's face. Maya said he must hide in the boot of the 7 League Boots to avoid any guards, and she drove so fast back to Reginald Xavier King that the wheels seemed not even to touch the ground nor people see them pass.

At the compound, she told King that for safety the Ogre's bank details were locked in the 7 League Boots in a hidden parking spot beyond the perimeter fence. She gave him a look that said she understood his game, and waited for the promised official documents giving safe passage to Europe for all her brothers and sisters.

On the great desk, lay a newspaper with a headline in large letters that read 'EU Ref: UK Votes Out', with a picture of tired looking people huddled in some sort of camp.

After a moment, King smiled, handed over a package containing official letters and new passports and followed Maya to the 7 League Boots.

The information was in a file under the back seat, she said. When King climbed in, she locked the door from the driver's seat, which was separated by a metal grill. Then as loud banging started from the boot and a startled look crossed King's face, Maya fired the powerful engine, pointed the 7 League Boots at the heavily guarded compound entry, jammed a rock on the accelerator, and released the handbrake as she leapt clear. All the soldiers saw was the blur of something big and very fast approaching, and they knew exactly what to do...

In the light of the ensuing fire and explosion, Maya looked at her package. On the boarding passes for the following day, for her and all her brothers and sisters, were the letters LHR, London Heathrow.

11

The cleaner and the banker

Nick Robins

It was late, but the vast trading floor was filled with sound. Not the raucous shouting of orders to buy and sell, but the sweet songs of home as Maria wiped the stains from the floor and emptied the bins. She sang so joyfully that you would think she had not a care in the world.

George was still at his desk, luxuriating over that day's miraculous trade. But he knew that he faced another sleepless night. Too much coffee perhaps, too much anxiety over the need to perform yet again the following day. He was even having nightmares – every time he fell asleep, Maria's idiotic songs would enter his head and wake him with a start.

How he wished that sleep was just another commodity, something he could just buy and sell. And when he couldn't sleep, he would just arrange stop-loss contract and so rest at last. Of course, a simpler solution was just to get Maria to cease her singing. So, he called her over and asked: "Maria, what do you earn each year from all this slaving away?"

Nervous with her English, Maria answered: "I have no idea, I don't think that far ahead, I simply work from day to day, hour by hour."

"Ok," said George. 'Then, what then do you make each day?"

"It's not that easy, Sir. Sometimes more, sometimes less, sometimes nothing when there are too many of us and I get nothing, zero, even if I'm ready to work."

"Let's not quibble over a few pennies," said George. "I'm a generous man – I'll give you the million pounds I made today. You'll never need to work again. It's small change for me, but like winning the Lottery for you."

George reached into his desk draw and handed Maria a golden coin, encrusted in diamonds. "Don't be afraid," he said. "It's genuine. I had it valued yesterday. It's worth a mill, what those stuffy Victorians would call a *marigold*, in fact."

Maria flushed red, embarrassed, hopeful, stunned – was this for real? This was more than she could earn in a lifetime of lifetimes.

"Just put your mark here," said George and he closed her fingers around a pen, sketching out her name on the top page of an impossibly tall document. Handing over the coin in a red velvet pouch, he walked her to the lifts.

Maria hurried home, avoiding the gaze of the other passengers on the night-bus and went straight to bed, putting the coin under her pillow.

But she couldn't sleep, terrified that she'd be accused of theft, or that someone would break in and steal the coin. When she finally got up, sticky with sweat, she noticed she was muttering to herself. She couldn't sing a note.

Worn out, she ran back to the bank and looked for George. There he was in the same place, but instead of his normal scowl, he was snoring.

Throwing down the coin onto his desk, she cried: "Here's your gold, take it and give back my songs. You can trade the world, but you can't buy me."

George woke slowly from his slumbers. "I'm afraid I can't do that. You see it's all in the contract you signed," he said, sounding bored and yet pleased with himself. "You have heard of derivatives, haven't you?"

Marygold or marigold is English slang meaning a million pounds. It is referenced by Brewer in 1870 but the origin is unclear, possibly related to the

Virgin Mary, and a style of church windows featuring her image. Story with apologies to La Fontaine's 'Cobbler'.

12

Bluebeard's cleaner

Molly Conisbee

In my opinion, he is a very self-contained man. It's very revealing being a cleaner for someone, because I always say that you see both the very best and very worst sides of human nature, doing this job. It's not all to do with money, either, although of course the people who can pay someone to clear up after them have got money. But prince or pauper, I always try and take people as I find them, and as I find them says a lot.

You ask how do I know he is self-contained, when I hardly see him? He works very long hours. I am not quite sure what he does for a living, I am not allowed in his office. Full of client details apparently, and I respect that. He has lots of lady friends, but it's so discrete. Please change the sheets he says, that's how I know, but they never leave a presence, no cotton wool or sanitary towels or spare toothbrushes in the bathroom.

My life, it's all in the mess people leave. It's the little things that really tell the story, that's what I always say. For example, if you wash a bathroom sink several times a day, like I do, you remember in your own bathroom sink not to let the blobs of toothpaste dry on the side of the bowl. It's a tiny thing, but if you leave it, it hardens and becomes a nightmare to scrub off. Same as used cereal bowls.

So at home, I get my lot to quickly rinse. Don't get me started in toilet manners. It's not like there's a poo fairy – except there is. That's me!

But he leaves no trace. So why does he bother with a cleaner? No blobs of toothpaste, no cereal bowls, no dirty pants on the floor, so stains on the cooker top, or God forbid, in the toilet bowl. Perhaps he leaves no reflection even, like a vampire!

As I said, he clearly has, shall we say, a lot of lady friends, but they never seem to last too long. He is what my son would call a 'commitment-phobe'. He keeps all the rooms in his house locked and it's such a hassle because I have to remember which key fits which room, and you'd think there'd be something special in there for all the paranoia about security. So he's like a dragon with its tail around treasure, but all that lies beyond is another clean room to clean! Except the office, of course. I can't go into the office.

Well, I shouldn't complain, should I, apart from

all the locked doors, it's an easy place to clean because it's so spotless, a quick job. When I was a chambermaid, we had time limits to how long we could spend cleaning a room, so you were taught how to hoover really quickly, leaving a kind of fan-shape on the floor so it looked like the whole thing had been more thoroughly done than it really had. That always troubled me a bit, somehow it felt like cheating, but we only had a few minutes per room, bathrooms and everything.

So I can't complain really. Mr Bluebeard is an excellent employer, one of my best. Pays on the nail. The house is clean and tidy and he's never awkwardly hanging around while I try and do my work. You couldn't ask for better really.

13

Peace and quiet

Nicky Saunter

He watched his wife dwindle to a tiny matchstick figure as she walked away around the harbour wall towards the paper shop, and felt a momentary sense of panic. Just a few weeks ago he would have felt only relief. And, once upon a time, he realised with sadness, he would have felt a sense of longing.

The bench faced the sun, one of many dotted along the seafront with square brass plaques in remembrance of 'Mum and Dad who loved this place so much'. Several wore a jaunty bouquet of wilting flowers in one corner, their plastic wrappers flapping in the breeze. When his time came, he hoped his wife would have better taste.

It was bright for November, but the wind was cold and he was well wrapped, sensible corduroy trousers and a thick sweater under his waterproof coat. People walked past him along the front chatting to each other, as their dogs scooted from post to post, lifting a leg, sniffing clumps of greenery. Some passers-by smiled and nodded in the companionable way of people at the seaside, but most looked quickly away when he failed to respond. Some showed pity or sympathy as he stared resolutely out to sea, fixing on the distant horizon with what he hoped appeared to be interest.

He could walk quite well now, even feed himself without too much spillage, and had even managed to urinate standing up without dripping on his trousers. But facial expressions were still impossible to predict and he was horrified, while looking in the mirror during his daily exercises, that his smile was the lopsided grimace of a B-movie lunatic. Speaking consisted of the occasional grunt at most, which took a huge amount of effort and was always disappointing for the recipient; it was easier to avoid people and thus embarrassment altogether.

The last time he had spoken to his wife was over six months ago. He had dropped her off at work after a normal enough journey; her usual litany of detail about people he barely knew and places he could not be bothered to remember, passing through him like some exotic torture that leaves no physical trace. His bored lack of response was a constant reproof. Better by far, he thought, than the constant bickering he heard between so many couples these days. On the rare occasions their silent battles descended into a more traditional shouting match, he exacted a secret revenge by picturing his wife struck with a rare and incurable disease that would leave her dumb.

He thought it funny how he had originally been drawn to this sensible, capable young woman who seemed to understand his need for silence, chatted easily for both of them at family get-togethers and listened reverently to his greater experience. But once married, he was not equipped for the relentless onslaught of intimacy, the simple attrition of living together day in, day out.

He withdrew gradually but steadily into his office, behind his newspaper and military history hardbacks. Her friends – and they were always *her* friends – visited less frequently and she spent her evenings catching up with them on the phone instead. She sought his intimacy less often and their conversations became increasingly one-sided. Twenty-seven years on, she continued to teach at the same school, cajoling and encouraging generations of other people's children, and had recently taken up Japanese flower arranging. He noticed fine lines appearing around her mouth as if she were permanently trying to draw it closed.

Work had dominated his life and it had suited him well. Forty-five years in insurance had ended quietly the week before with a discreet gathering and a year's membership to the local golf club. He couldn't wait for it to expire. But when his wife asked him for the date of his last day at work – she wanted to write it on the calendar and organise a small luncheon for him, nothing showy and no ghastly surprises – he had shocked himself by giving the date of the Friday a week later.

He felt there was no harm in his dissembling; just a need to be alone, to savour some peace and quiet. At first, he fantasised about doing something important and meaningful – something he would remember for the rest of his life. After all, the Sunday papers regularly featured apparently normal people who used their retirement to canoe the Atlantic or feed gorillas in Rwanda. This seemed unnecessarily showy to him, but he understood their basic desire to step outside their daily life.

But as the day approached, he was paralysed with indecision and instead, he dressed simply for work, left the house at the usual time, and drove out of town, following the long estuary to the seaside near to where he spent his holidays as a child. He walked for miles along the coastal path looking down on lonely coves and crashing waves.

He repeated this for the next few days, delighting in the isolation and nostalgia, until he found himself in a windswept car park near the pier on Friday afternoon, suddenly and inexplicably wanting to go home. This was when he had the stroke that would have killed him if it had not been for the sharp-eyed ice cream man who saw him fall on the wet gravel, and happened to be a first aider.

He was lucky to be alive, said the local paper, as they interviewed his rescuer. His wife had no idea why he was there, they reported. A nervous breakdown? An affair?

When she read that he had retired a week earlier, she cried through a whole box of tissues in her room, mystified and smarting. Still, she thought it was the most interesting thing her husband had ever done. She had promised herself that, if he recovered, she would confront him directly with his hurtful subterfuge, but the opportunity seemed to slip away and the idea now seemed faintly ridiculous.

The stroke unit thought he would eventually make a good physical recovery but it seemed increasingly unlikely that his speech would return. Aphasia, they called it; an inability to speak. He had heard of people with strokes misplacing words, mangling sentences, and even someone who shouted "Basketry" at regular intervals, but he always pictured them as dribbling and incapacitated. This was something quite different: the indignity of understanding a conversation but being completely unable to participate. His wife encouraged him to make gestures or drawings, but he found this humiliating and he was spectacularly bad at it.

A large seagull skimmed across the last few breakers and landed effortlessly on the harbour wall, its wings folding invisibly into its smooth flanks. The wind was whipping his scarf and, although he could move his hands quite well now, he struggled to grasp the flapping cloth and tuck it back inside his coat.

"The wind can be so very annoying, innit?" said a rather high, rasping voice from immediately in front of him. It broke immediately into bursts of high, grating laughter.

Brian looked to his left and saw only an elderly couple several benches away, the women laboriously unscrewing the lid from a thermos flask. To his right was a young woman standing some way away, staring out to sea and listening to music on her headphones. In front of him, the seagull fixed its shiny black eyes on him and shifted its weight threateningly from one orange skinny leg to the other.

"Mind you, it's worth it for the thermals. Riding a big one on a warm day is a fine experiential, mark my worms."Brian looked at the gull, so much larger than it had appeared in flight, a muscular bird with improbably precise markings on its bill and neck in crisp white, grey and black.

The hairs rose on the back of his neck and his heart began to whoosh uncomfortably in his ears. He was going mad or gulls were starting to speak an unusual dialect of English, or perhaps he had fallen asleep and was just dreaming vividly.

A tall man appeared suddenly from behind the bench, hesitated and then walked briskly off down the path to the right. Brian felt ridiculous and relieved at once. The voice must have been his. He felt his chest lift and his lungs fill properly with air as he laughed out loud. The noise felt strange coming out of his mouth, like the honk of a goose.

"My, my! You do sound poorly, ducks. Not getting much in the way of laughs these days?" The seagull's head was slightly inclined and its beak a fraction open. Looking wildly around him, Brian realised with an increasing sense of unreality that there was now no one within earshot.

Oh my God, thought Brian, *I've had a stroke, I can't speak and now I'm imagining that seagulls can talk.*

"Got any chips?"

No I haven't. How can you hear me? I can't

speak, you know.

"Samwidges?"

Sandwiches. No! Anyway, shouldn't you be eating fish? Junk food is bad for wildlife, you know.

"Looks like I should really be taking advice from you about healthy eating, ole man!"

The bird's eyes narrowed and it pulled its chin in, moving back and forth. "Anyway, chips are perfect for eating by the sea – especially those little crispy bits. So where's your mate, mate? Or have you been abandoned? Ha ha."

No I have not. My wife has just gone to get me a newspaper. He wondered for a brief moment what he would do if she had in fact finally given in to his constantly stated wish for solitude and had simply walked away out of his life.

You still haven't told me how you can understand what I am thinking.

"No idea, matey. Sometimes no-fly peoples can hear you; sometimes they can't. Thinking, blinking, talking, squawking – s'all the same to me, me old mate. Saw you sitting here looking like a crumpled old chip paper. Thought perhaps you were on your toddle. Molly coddle – ha ha. Need a bit of cheering up, up and away. Know what I mean?"

Yes. I mean that's very kind of you, but I am fine, thank you.

"Don't look fine to me. I know a peoples look when they're down on their stumps. I was serious bad potato when my mate didn't come back. Terrible times they were – waited for weeks, kept going back to the nest but she never showed. Lost at sea, you see." The seagull paced slowly up and down the wall, looking out to sea.

Brian thought momentarily of Maggie flying out to sea, never to return. He felt a lump rising in his throat and his eyes began to sting with tears. What was happening to him?

I'm so sorry, had you known her long?

"Mated for life, mate," said the gull, fixing him with one black shiny eyeball. Then he lifted his wings slightly, resettling them more comfortably. "Only joking, boyo – plenty more fish in the sea, plenty more gulls in the sky. Got any chips?"

No I haven't got any bloody chips! Brian felt shocked and inexplicably upset.

"Keep your hair on matey-o!" the bird drew back on the wall as if Brian had attacked him. "Life's a lark and then you fly! Nice to toot the breezes with you – but I must be off. Waves to skim, icey cremos to steal, peoples to annoy. Ha ha."

With that, he lifted his huge wings out to the wind and rose sideways like an ice-skater into the air. Within seconds, he had mingled with the other gulls, flying to and fro across the harbour in ever-changing patterns, criss-crossing the sky with their questioning eyebrow silhouettes.

"I'm sorry I was so long – they had run out of *The Times* so I had to go along to the parade". He felt Maggie's hand on his shoulder and she sat down beside him, slightly out of breath. "Oh, Brian - are you all right? Shall we go home – you look terrible."

Brian turned to look at his wife, her face creased with worry and her eyes searching his, seeking a reply and yet expecting none. His lips trembled, moving tentatively as he sought the air to force out a sound.

"Gull," he said.

14

Erysichthon

Geoff Mead

Mestra was nearly 60, though looking at her it was hard to tell her age. Her chestnut hair, streaked with grey, was thick and lustrous; her dark blue eyes were clear and sparkling; the contours of her face – marked with the softest of lines – shifted with every change in the light.

The day was hot and the rippling waves in the bay below scattered the sun's iridescent reflection onto the plastered ceiling and walls of the guest room of the old palace, making the painted dolphins seem to swim in their painted sea. Mestra turned to the young man sitting opposite her, his eyes on the horizon, and smiled:

"Odysseus, you've done nothing for weeks but sit on that stool and stare out to sea."

"What else is there to do, Grandmother, until my leg heals and I can go home to Ithaka?" said her grandson, stroking his bandaged thigh. "Besides, I love the sea."

"It must run in the family," said Mestra. "Poseidon was my first love too. I couldn't stay out of the water when I was a girl. I was a good swimmer then, almost as good as those dolphins on the wall."

She laughed – a deep chuckle – like the sound of gurgling water. "And if I wasn't swimming, I was lying on the beach, daydreaming about what it would be like to float like a jellyfish or fly like a seagull or dart like a sand eel."

Odysseus gazed at his grandmother and tried to imagine her as she might have been at his own age. There were family rumours about her – that she had lived a far from ordinary life – but this was his first visit to his grandparent's realm and he realized that he knew very little about her past.

"Tell me about your life, Grandmother," he said. "I shall be king in Ithaka one day and a king should know his lineage. Tell me your story."

"Your grandfather has all the best stories," she replied. "He'll make you laugh. You don't want to listen to me; my story is too dark for a day like this."

"Light or dark, it's all the same to me," said Odysseus. "I'm curious about the whole world. I want to know everything."

"If you're sure," said Mestra, suddenly serious. "But I don't think you'll like it. Not all your ancestors pleased the gods or covered themselves with glory. You asked me to tell you my story but, to do that, I must tell you the story of my father – your great-grandfather."

She paused for a moment to steady herself and gather her thoughts, before launching into her tale.

"Things began well enough. He was born a prince: the only son of Tropias, king of Thessaly. But his parents spoiled him and he grew up too used to getting his own way. Most young men are selfish but he got more arrogant and demanding with each year that passed. One day, he took it into his head to build a banqueting hall for himself and his companions. It would be the most splendid hall ever built, made from the rarest stone and finest timber.

"When it was time to raise the roof, he took twenty woodsmen – armed with double-axes – to a grove of trees that was well-known to be sacred to the goddess Demeter. Pine and elm, oak and ash, apple and pear grew so close together that an arrow would scarcely have passed between them. At the centre stood a great oak, strung with garlands and wreaths, towering above the rest. It caught his eye at once. 'Cut it down,' he commanded.

"The woodsmen stood back afraid to touch the holy tree. Your grandfather seized an axe and swung the first blow himself. It's said that the tree shuddered and groaned, and that blood poured out of the wound like the lifeblood that gushes from the throat of a bull sacrificed at the altar. The branches of the oak trembled and every leaf and acorn grew pale. 'Stop this impious act,' said one of the woodsmen, braver than the rest. 'Can't you see that you are offending the goddess herself?'

"Perhaps, if my father had stopped then, he might have been able to make amends. But that was not his way. 'Take that for your piety,' he cried and applied his axe to the protestor's neck. No-one else dared oppose him and blow by blow they hacked at the shrieking tree until it crashed to the ground."

Horrified by the images her words had conjured, Mestra fell silent. She touched her forehead with her right hand and cast her eyes up to heaven as if to remind the gods that it was her father who had committed this sacrilege and that she was just the storyteller.

"Then what happened?" prompted Odysseus.

"What happened? My father was doomed from that moment on," said Mestra. "The gods intervened, but we can only surmise what the gods actually do: we are like dry leaves whirling in the wind they create as they pass through our lives. I will tell you what I know and what I have been told by those wiser than myself.

"The men cut the sacred tree into stout lengths of timber and took them back to the palace to complete the new banqueting hall. It was indeed a splendid building but no feast was ever held there, no bards ever sung under its roof, and no guests ever entered its magnificent doors.

"The day after the hall was finished, my father woke up with a fierce gnawing hunger that could not be satisfied. He went straight to the palace kitchens and began to eat everything in sight: bread, meat, fish, poultry, pastries, fruit, vegetables, grain, and even raw offal. He ate and ate and would not, could not, stop. When the kitchen was empty, he ate the larder bare. When he had shovelled the contents of the larder down his gullet and drunk the store of wine dry, he went out into the yard and set his teeth into the heifer, the donkey and the cat. But the more he ate, the hungrier he became."

Odysseus stared at Mestra, wide-eyed.

"The priestess told my grandmother that Demeter was so infuriated by the desecration of her grove that she sent a nymph to the bare mountain top in Scythia, where gaunt Hunger prowls, to bid her visit my father at night, wrap her bony arms around him, put her toothless gums to his mouth and send her stinking breath coursing through his veins. The priestess must have spoken the truth because my father's appetite could not be satisfied.

"In the weeks and months that followed, entire flocks of sheep and goats were slaughtered, herds of prime cattle put to the knife, whole orchards and vineyards stripped of their fruit, granaries and storehouses emptied; hoards of silver, gold, and bronze exchanged for food. The very stones and timbers of the palace itself were traded for anything that could be eaten. My father's banqueting hall was the only royal building left intact. No-one dared to touch it, in case they too suffered Demeter's wrath.

"No amount of food or drink could diminish his titanic craving or nourish his aching body. He became more like a ghost than a man: his flesh withered until his arms and legs were no more than bone and sinew. His ribs rattled when he breathed. His wild eyes stared out of hollow sockets. His parents, friends, servants, even his wife – my mother – deserted him.

"Only I remained and I could hardly bear to see him. I stayed out of his way as much as I could, but when he had chomped his way through every last edible morsel in the kingdom and guzzled the last drop of wine, he called me to him."

Odysseus stared wide-eyed at his grandmother: "He didn't try to eat you too, did he?"

"No," said Mestra. "But what he had in mind was

almost as bad. He sold me as a slave to a passing merchant to get money to buy more food."

"Outrageous," said Odysseus through gritted teeth. "It's outrageous that one of my ancestors should do such a thing. How did the merchant treat you?"

"Well, you could say that the merchant got more – or rather that he got less – than he bargained for. As soon as we were alone, I started crying out to Poseidon, as if he were my lover. I wriggled my body like a fish; I curled and uncurled like a seahorse; I gulped the air as if I had gills. In short, I made the merchant think that I was quite mad. The girl he had bought disappeared and in her place was a creature of the sea. He let me go and I went home and begged my father to leave me in peace.

"But when I told him how I had escaped, he realized that this trick was too good not to repeat. He sold me again and again and each time I feigned madness to escape: I mooed, tossed my head and stamped my feet and the girl disappeared, changed into a cow; I became a horse, a dog, even a parrot.

"But the little he got from selling me was not enough to keep his cavernous stomach filled. He took to begging at crossroads for leavings and scraps of food. I realized that nothing I could do would save him and I couldn't bear to watch my father dwindle and die. I was desperate to get away.

"When your grandfather Autolycus came along, I allowed myself to be sold one last time. I made no effort to escape. I had had enough and I was happy to go with him. He would probably tell you that he bought me for a handful of silver but the truth is that I liked the look of him. He made me his queen and he's never given me cause to regret my decision. He's a decent man, despite his reputation for being a rogue. I think we both got a good bargain."

"Well I'm certainly glad you found each other," said Odysseus, "or I wouldn't be here. But what happened to your father?"

"Word came to us that his half-eaten corpse was found by the crossroads. I can hardly bring myself to speak of it but they say that he died attempting to devour his own body. That was the terrible end meted out by the gods to your great-grandfather Erysichthon – the 'earth-tearer' – as a warning to anyone whose greed despoils the land.

"My father turned his kingdom into a wasteland, but the banqueting hall still stands, I'm told. Its stones are covered in ivy now and green shoots have sprung from the roof timbers. Demeter is taking back what is hers and should never have been taken from her."

Mestra and her grandson sat quietly for a while,

until their reverie was broken by the sound of a pack of dogs baying as they neared the palace after the day's hunt. "Autolycus will be home soon," Mestra said, to break the spell of the story.

"Are we cursed?" asked Odysseus. "Did Erysichthon's crime condemn us too? Can a family ever be free of such a thing?"

"My father paid in full for what he did. Our fortunes are ours to make or mar. The gods will judge us by our own actions, not those of our forbears. We have neither license nor excuse for the choices we make."

Mestra rose from her stool and walked over to her grandson. She took his head in both hands and kissed his forehead. "I am going outside to greet my husband when he returns," she said. "Stay here and look at the sea some more. You are healing quickly; soon you will be well enough to sail back home and the adventure of your life will truly begin."

She released Odysseus from her embrace and strode out of the room. "I won't disgrace you, Grandmother," he called after her, his eyes returning to the horizon. "I will tread lightly upon this earth, I promise you."

15

After the oil harbour

Rina Kuusipalo

The sea was furious at the end of the summer, tossing dark moss-coloured waves onto the shore as if to salvage itself. A distant red sun was melting into the far horizon like burning liquid iron, painting the sky crimson. Far away, pine woods and olive groves decorated the hillside, humming with the steady beat of crickets. Along the coast, large white cylinders and rusted capsized tankers the size of villages dotted the shoreline. Bear watched pieces of driftwood hitting the sand. Door frames, books, umbrellas, shoes, relics from an everyday.

Behind a dune, Wolf dug. Feverishly, she shovelled heaps of sand onto the side of a hole, with sweat running down her forehead into her eyes making her squint. Crabs crawled out, glistening in the sunlight for a while, casting sharp shadows, and then vanishing back into the dunes. She caught some in her grip and placed them in a bucket. Their claws clattered against the metal. Wolf suddenly felt nauseous.

All week, they had been eating the crabs and it was not good. They had been delighted to find protein-rich food, other than crickets, nuts, and seeds. Then, some toxins in the crabmeat had begun to affect her, she was sure, because she had begun imagining their dangly legs scuttling through her intestines, in the darkness of beating organs, eating on a liver she knew was poisoned.

You had to be extremely careful with food after the Disaster. It was a daily trade-off between hunger and tumours. Apart from the floods, droughts, wars, and storms, it was illness that had eventually taken most. Now the shovel struck into the heavy black substance that tarred the subsoil along the shore: thick oil simmering in the sun, dripping off the shovel in slow motion. Everywhere she dug, more oil. Nowhere to go.

Hot from sweat, Wolf threw her clothes into a bush. She stepped into the sea and dived in, escaping from the putrid foam on the surface.

The dive into the unknown is a lonely, holy dive, a death of sorts, she thought, searching the murky landscape for anything living. Her eyes burned but she wanted to see, even though everyone told her there were no more fish here. This diving, even if futile and damaging to her health, as Bear kept saying, was a practice of the mind for what would come and for what had been. Here she could feel like a speck of comet looking upon a vastness full of possibility, could lose sense of time, could surface looking at the world from a distance, and could remember how breakable it was.

Emerging now, Wolf looked up at the sky, red and effervescent, a blood-red reminiscent of living bodies. The sun had almost disappeared. The birds were flying low; it was going to rain soon. They would need to find shelter for this rain burned like acid. Tears welled up in her eyes. She found herself thinking of Snow again.

It had been many years but she could not let go. Maybe Bear was right, that love should not transform itself into this ruminating kind of wallowing with no end in sight, this abyss of introspection, this tar-like substance that swelled up inside, filling every corner and drowning moments of potential into a grey blur. But although she wished it had, the new world had not made her stoic. Bear, on the other hand, always adapted so calmly, unruffled by it all.

Bear sat watching Wolf. She was foolish to swim, no doubt. Yet, he, too, would have liked to dive into the water and look with eyes wide open. He wondered how she was able to spend whole minutes underwater. Though it irritated him at times, he envied her stubborn will to find something, to never stop searching. She was more fearless than him at the core. The truth was that he was now so afraid of losing people and things he hoped for, that he allowed himself to desire nothing. Besides, he could not withstand the silence of dead fish littered across the seafloor and the smell of poison above.

Wolf was crying now. She never hid her tears. Bear never cried, not in front of anyone. He wanted to tell her that the weight of loss did not have to overtake her. She should gather distance from what was, but was the kind of person who absorbed the pain of others and gave large parts of herself to those around her. Yet she did so too readily and hastily, as if she did not realise the habit created caverns in her that would ache when the holder of the part was gone. And so many were gone now, dead or disappeared into a world with few possibilities of finding each other again. She had to accept that nothing could be trusted to last. They had to move along alone, or in shared solitude. It was dark now; no stars, just an eternal blanket of fog.

Bear was nonetheless a believer of sorts. He believed in the theory held by many survivors that mimicking the mind-sets of different animals could allow you to survive, to live without spite and hate, to let go of grief, and to be alert to the current moment and the ones to come, not those past. Good could only be caught in glimpses, colours burnt on the retina for a moment, then faded.

Bear also remembered that, when he was young, his cousin's dog lay by the grave of her dead owner for months, refusing food, until she starved. He had rarely seen a human mourn with such conviction.

"What is this?" Wolf shouted, standing in the waves, tossing the foam away.

As her body moved in the water, something was coming alive underneath the blackness. Bright flickers of light followed her movement wherever her limbs crossed, illuminating the seabed. The creatures, whatever they were, gleamed blindingly in the dark like the starry skies that were.

For a while, Wolf was filled with a sense of something she could only call magic. She could not say that word, could not speak of the dreamlike, because Bear, who still bore the legacy of cultivated rational thinking, would laugh. But wild weeds germinated still. She had not been paying due attention. But, this was a reminder of something underneath the surface, of things between the lines.

Bear stood quiet for a while. "It is plankton, bioluminescent plankton," he said. "Inedible."

Inside, however, Bear too was amazed. He was startled that anything might live in this toxic water. Did this mean other things could also have survived? He had only ever seen pictures of such plankton while staring at his computer screen in some electrically-lit building procrastinating over *National Geographic* pictures of 'Most Beautiful Places to Visit.'

Once he could afford to visit such places, but never did. Now, he had no money. There was no money, only barter for insect paste. Yet here he was, feeling small above the gaze of the lit-up sea like a child. He had been a madman rummaging numbers, running in meaningless circles like a hamster on a wheel. He had been shaking with fear at night when the running stopped, an insomniac. It was Wolf who eventually taught him to sleep for whole nights. Recently, he had begun dreaming. But he did not tell her; she would look for ridiculous meanings in his dreams.

Eventually, when the rain clouds gathered, Wolf returned to shore. They found shelter in a shop near the beach, shelves dusty and emptied long ago except for a corner with sunglasses, deflated beach toys, and magazines from seven years ago. As the rain poured outside, dimming colour, Bear fell asleep.

Wolf stayed awake listening to the rattle of rain on the tin roof. It was her turn to keep watch.

Years ago, when Snow died, it had also rained like this. Sheets of snow hovered from the skies that afternoon, waltzing on the wind, before descending to their death. From the blanket of clouds rain began seeping, coloured purple by the haze that was enveloping the earth.

It was then that Snow spoke to her.

We will all have to flee. We will all be in exile. Did we think we would be spared, that we would be special and invulnerable, when trees, animals, and other people fell around us? The ocean is boiling and raging. Dark unnatural clouds litter the sky and the water keeps rising.

They tell me there was no way to foresee these events. I told them about the rocks and the winds and the ice and the animals and the plants and the people that communicated signs long ago. They told me to speak in another tongue, a proper tongue, to give them evidence on paper.

So we gave them paper, filled their offices with calculations and reports, precise in every way possible. But still they claimed they could not imagine a way to change. When others did, they silenced them.

But was the new so different from the old as to be unimaginable? Fine balance was required then, as it is now. The diseases have been reborn, unfrozen from our permafrost, and our reindeer have all been slaughtered. A fine balance is required.

Archive our grammars into your innermost tissue if written word should ever fail. When you leave these barren hills of lichen, the land of the Saami, and when I am gone, you will forget, so carry shards with you – shards so sharp that they will pierce your heart if it begins to freeze.

They are stories that will light raging northern lights in your chest. In the calculated days, hovering lamps in corridors lit your way as your value passed through the verdict of rooms full of manmade things. But that now changes. How I wish the change had not come like this, so violently. Change could have meant birth, not destruction.

There is no 'I' that I can speak as anymore. I am losing my form and correspondence to reality now . But remember what I was   : not one but many   , skoavdi, čahki, gaska-skárta, seaŋaš, njáhcu, goahpálat, guoldu, luotkku, moarri, ruokŋa, skárta, skávvi...[1]

Wolf was stirred from half-sleep by the sensation of a wet tile floor against her cheek. Rainwater was flooding the shop. She woke up Bear and they stepped outside. The water was rising and they would need to relocate.

They fetched their backpacks and got on their bicycles, old but well-oiled from the olives they had squeezed, and cycled inland. The pinewoods surrounded them, providing shelter as they glided under the large unfolding treetops.

"At Academy, they taught us that nothing lives inside the woody bark of a tree," Bear remarked, pedalling and wiping off rain from his forehead. "They told us that the human chest contains the only consciousness in the universe."

"Do you believe that?" Wolf asked.

"I used to," he said.

The road forked and they took the steep path leading uphill.

---

[1]*"Diversity in Saami terminology for reindeer and snow," Ole Henrik Magga, Professor of Saami Linguistics, Saami University College in Guovdageaidnu, Norway.*

"Too heavy to pedal," Bear gasped, and they stopped to walk the bicycles.

"But really," Bear continued, "I spent years studying applied biochemistry, so I try to apply it. Thought and compassion seem to be rippled obstinately wherever pain is felt, even where we cannot grasp how that pain is felt. With some organisms, our pain seems almost identical. With others, it is beyond our own wavelength, but that doesn't mean it isn't there."

Bear grabbed a twig off the pine and chewed on the needles. "We know that these pines communicate with each other through their roots, that was detected through science. But to imagine what goes on beyond those rudimentary electrical sensors..."

The path ended at a gate that was shut and a ramshackle house in the distance. They stood in silence by the roadside for a while. A shadow had grown on Wolf's face.

"Should we?" she asked, hesitantly. Wolf was happy to sleep in the forest where she could hear her surroundings and run if needed, but she preferred to inspect buildings during the day before spending a night. But it was still raining.

"Come on," Bear said. "It looks empty. And you have to let go of your fear of strangers."

"I'm not afraid. I'm just being careful with good

reason. Let's just sleep in the forest. I need nothing but the forest. I can lie down under the trees and the ugly sky all day, just reading and smoking."

"Can't smoke in the rain now," Bear said.

Wolf ignored him "We carry nothing anyone can steal, it is rarely cold, so for what do we need the building? There is plenty of stuff in the world and what is missing is society, company. So why would someone ruin their chance to make a friend in this lonely place for want of some scrappy utensils, a can of beans, for a rusty bike."

"All the more reason to knock on the door," Bear said.

"I do think people are fundamentally hospitable," Wolf said, "unless in want. But many are nowadays."

"And if they are in want, we share with them, and the tension dissipates," Bear said. "Of course, there are the unkind ones. But haven't there always been the unkind ones."

"Fine," Wolf said. "But it is on you if this is an unkind house."

They opened the gate and walked to the door, knocking a few times. They heard ruffling and steps.

"Someone is inside. I told you," Wolf whispered.

"Too late to turn back now," Bear whispered, and announced: "We are looking for shelter from the rain."

An old woman with round spectacles and dishevelled white hair peered through the window. "No speak English." She opened the door and whispered to someone behind here. A boy, perhaps ten years old, appeared and said: "My grandmother asks if you are English."

"No, no. I was from Egypt," Bear said, pointing to himself. "She was from Lapland."

Giulia nodded.

"You can stay," the boy said. "Sorry. The English turned our family away, so she doesn't like them."

"We are so grateful," Wolf said. "Thank you."

Pointing to herself, the old woman said: "Giulia," and pointing to the boy, she said: "Romulus. No madre, no padre." The boy looked away.

Wolf and Bear ended up staying with Giulia and Romulus for several weeks. They helped grow and gather food – wheat, olives, insects, pine kernels, vegetables, mushrooms, tomatoes. They tried to teach Romulus how to hunt animals but he said he could survive without. They learnt that Romulus's parents and sister had died while fleeing the mudslides. He never spoke about it.

hen a new group arrived, a family of four, Wolf and Bear decided to continue travelling. Everyone was on the move. Everyone had loved ones they were looking for. Moving made it seem as though you might find them, at least traces of them.

During their last night at the house, Wolf and Bear slept in the forest to make space for the others. They listened to the wind and the rustling of branches in the darkness.

"You're afraid of houses. But aren't you afraid of the sounds of creatures in the forest at night?" Bear asked.

"When I don't hear these sounds anymore," Wolf said, "then I will be afraid."

16

The child from a modest star

Lindsay Mackie

"How hard it is to set aside
Terror, concupiscence and pride,
Learn who and where we are,
The children of a modest star."
From *New Year Letter*, W.H. Auden

"I think I'd like to visit Earth," said the child.

"It's a long way and we are not sure what you will find," said the Elders.

"But I can just wish myself there," the child said. "And, I want to find an answer."

From this modest star, so far away that no spaceship has visited or even has it on GPS, citizens have the choice to go wandering when they are a certain age. Not very old, but old enough to think for themselves, which everyone from the modest star can do.

It was considered good and interesting for citizens to look outside their circular perimeters, the golden skies and airy glades which make up the modest star. They do love to visit. Not all go, but of all who do, all return. They journey to galaxies, stars, meteors, they dive through clouds and head for the suns. Not too close, but much closer than we could endure.

They don't take much along, maybe a cuddly toy. But they are always furnished with two things:

The wish, which will get them back in a twinkling from wherever to the modest star.

And the Magic Coat. That's what they call it, but in reality it is neither magic nor a coat. It's more of an attitude. It allows them to understand another living thing with such delicacy and detail that they become like that thing. They become indistinguishable from the rest of that species.

There is a catch (well, when is there not? I ask you? Even worse, there are in fact *two* catches). There is only one wish, and the Magic Coat cannot be used selfishly. The Elders are most particular about this. So if you want just to see what it's like to be a tiger or a wasp, just for interest or fun or to tell your pals an amazing story, then it's a 'no'. And, instead, you will suffer an nasty attack of pimples for at least an hour.

The child was excited. No doubt about that. She watched from her eyrie the blue orb of earth circling lazily through its galaxy. It was beautiful. Who would she meet there? What friends? What music would she hear? What would she learn (which was the aim of this wandering for as long as it had existed).

The Elders set it all up. A farewell ceremony. The golden air more golden. The glades more soft and green. The citizens more loving. Then – WHOOSH!

You might imagine a bump, a breathless looking around, a 'where am I'.

But it wasn't at all like that. The child had planned her location with care and she tapped, as it were, the Magic Coat a second before she landed on the green grass of the school playing field. The game was football and it was fast and furious. The child was impressed. There was a long exciting kick. The child clapped. Then another long, exciting kick back in the opposite direction. The child clapped again.

The boys standing next to her looked cross. "Make you mind up. Which team are you for?" The child felt something awful in her stomach. Anger, that's what it was. She wished she could not feel what the boys were feeling.

Luckily, just at that moment, there was a goal. The boys were thrilled. The child consulted her itinerary. Time to move on – WHOOSH!

It had been raining in the valley. There was that soft enveloping mistiness that clears as soon as the sun appears. In the middle of a nearby field, two hares were leaping and dancing. The gamekeeper was standing by the gate. He had a gun on his shoulder. The child – remember the Magic Coat - was wearing a tweed jacket and an old holey sweater and she had a deep voice.

"Those hares are enjoying themselves."

The gamekeeper agreed. "There are more of them this year because of the rain. It's been too wet for the grass to be cut for silage so the leverets haven't be cut down by the blades."

WHAT?

But the child merely nodded. She looked at the glades and the fields, and the mountains in the west and the hares and the man, and she thought: "I can't stay here. This is not what I am looking for."

WHOOSH!

The child had heard about the ways in which people on Earth communicated. It seemed primitive – tablets held to the ear, loud rings, cries of 'Hello, hello, you're breaking up'. She thought of the cave paintings on her modest star, where the scholars had more or less definitely worked out that her own ancestors – so long ago – had used similar means of calling across the great lakes and plains of the old world.

So she settled herself into the call centre of a phone company. Here she might find that another planet had the same joy in understanding each other that she and the citizens had!

Well, you can guess how that worked out. The child began to wish she had spent more time at the football match. At least the game was lovely, and the anger and suspicion and frustration were less.

EVERYONE WAS FURIOUS. Their phones didn't work. They were being scammed. There was no reception. What were you going to do about it? Perhaps, thought the child, they don't really want to communicate. Or perhaps they just don't want to be alone but don't know how to communicate.

Here I am, thought the child, as she body-swerved a giant supermarket entrance with tired people coming in and out. I am on Earth and I am looking for the person who will let me know that we are not alone on the modest star. There are others like us. We who are kind and, as our name suggests, modest in our needs. Careful with our planet, and loving to our trees and grass and animals.

I do need to know we are not alone, thought the child, though she didn't know quite why she needed to know this. Just then a small girl with a dog came up to her. "My mum's in the supermarket," she said. "I have to watch our dog. He gets really anxious if we leave him. So we have to take him everywhere. You can pat him if you like."

The child patted the dog. "He's really sweet," she said.

The small girl nodded. "We rescued him. From a rescue centre. My mum stayed up with him for three nights till he calmed down. My mum says we will never let him down. She says letting people down is awful and it's awful for dogs too. She says it makes you into a Dickhead."

The child looked at her. I've found it, she thought. I can go back now and tell them, tell the Elders: It's true, there is Life on Earth.

WHOOSH!

17

What the long, red-legged scissorman did next

Rob Hopkins

The long, red-legged scissorman was enjoying the feeling of the sunshine on the back of his neck as he weeded. Hairy bittercress, groundsel and ragged robin were eased from the soil and tossed into the bucket at his side. The No.87 bus had just pulled out from the bus stop whose shadow fell close to where he worked, and already mothers with children and other travellers were beginning to gather for the next bus. The bustle of a London weekday looked better, felt less impersonal, when viewed through a low screen of plants. The scissorman leant back onto his ankles and looked around.

Hops, almost ready to pick, and heady with their lupulin aromas, rambled over the fence. Chard, kale and onions stood out in the beds where he worked. Further away were mixes of flowers and soft fruits.

The sunlight illuminated the colours of the different varieties of chard like stained glass.

Thirty years ago, life had been very different. In the five years before his long prison sentence, the long, red-legged scissorman's reign of terror became the stuff of legend. His intolerance for what he perceived as badly behaved children led him to do some terrible things. While his day job as a tailor kept him busy, his scissors also deprived many children of their thumbs, first a child named Conrad, but then, as he became emboldened – "snip, snap, snip", his scissors would go, his punishment for children who sucked their thumbs. He really was an intolerant bastard in those days.

Back then, times were different. Children were meant to be seen and not heard. Biting your nails, not putting your knife and fork together after eating, speaking out of turn, were all sufficient grounds for punishment. Then, the long, red-legged scissorman hated kids. He hated everyone in fact. He hated being a tailor. The world was not a place of beauty, of laughter, of kindness. It was an untidy, chaotic and disordered place that needed to be taught some manners. It all caught up with him, of course.

Although he was initially celebrated as some kind of hero by commentators, who thrived on intolerance (the book celebrating his actions, *Struwwelpeter*, became a best-seller), and the right wing media dubbed him the 'Manners Vigilante', the public mood rapidly shifted, and his regular de-thumbing of children led to his arrest, trial, and eventual imprisonment. Conrad's mother lost custody of her son when, rather than being shocked at what had occurred, she simply told social workers: "I knew he'd come, to naughty little Suck-a-Thumb".

It was a Thursday, a day he still remembered with great clarity. He had been taking a bus journey back to his flat. Recently released from prison, he had chosen not to return to tailoring, but started an access course with an eye perhaps to going into engineering.

His bus pulled into Gresham Lane bus stop, a stop he hadn't alighted at before. As he stepped out, he realised this was no ordinary bus stop. Around it had been built a garden, a food garden. It was being tended by three people, who were at that moment planting out salads. A bus stop that grows food? Something fused in his mind.

He read the sign on the bus stop. Apparently it was an 'Edible Bus Stop', one of eight along that particular route. The bus station at the start of the route was, apparently, the city's first Edible Bus

Station. Local people had come together and turned grim places into beautiful living spaces, producing food that anyone passing buy was welcome to help themselves to.

He sat nearby and watched. He noticed that something unusual happened to the children who came to wait for buses. The garden held their attention, delighted them. Children seemed somehow calmer than at the bus stop near his flat. Their parents did too. He engaged the salad planters in conversation, and soon found himself helping out, planting out three trays of spring onions.

He had come to see this labour as his life's work: this healing of unloved and damaged places, this bringing of kindness and peace to neglected and troubled corners that most people were happier to just walk past. It somehow healed the unloved and damaged places inside himself, bringing kindness and peace to the corners of his being that he had tried to run away from.

He travelled the land, carrying little more than a notebook and a toothbrush in his small red backpack, visiting 'Fruity Corners' in Lancaster, 'Incredible Edible Todmorden' in Yorkshire, with its food gardens up the high street and around the police station, and urban gardens from Glasgow to Brighton, from Penzance to Norwich. In every one of them, in spite of their diversity, their different people and settings, he found the same spirit, the same sense of people coming home to the place, to each other.

He felt something shifting around him. In many gardens, young people came to learn new skills, to be outside, to unwind. Rather than being mannerless wild beasts in need of taming, he came to see them as thoughtful, sometimes lost, souls rather like him, and that he had skills to offer them. Gone, he realised with delight, were the days when de-thumbing young people for sucking their thumbs, or celebrating their misfortune, were acceptable. Yes, he thought, these are troubled times, but our tolerance, our compassion, our kindness, is growing, and is vital.

Ten years later, when he was elected Mayor of London, his vision of the city as a Farm City became that of the citizens too, with houses spread among the vast farm, thriving with intensive food growing and new businesses, a generation of young people now with access to good, affordable food. It became an infectious vision, spreading to cities around the world. He based his policies on the needs of mothers and children, arguing that what worked for them would, by necessity, work for everyone else.

He could see the gardens that were growing inside his own heart spread, and take root in many other places.

18

Little Red

Andrew Simms

His stomach lurched at the smell of hot alarm drifting through the woods. Eynar suppressed the impulse to flee. Although familiar, it was different to the burnt and bitter wisps he remembered from years before. They had been early warnings of forest fire.

Back then, his father's sense of smell was failing with age. He'd realized too late that the fire was encircling him. Eynar and his family mourned his loss to the smoke and flames for a long time. Not until the winter months did their minds turn back to concerns for their own survival.

This new smell that made him twist inside wasn't to be feared in the same way as the crackling rage that reshaped the forest once a generation. But he knew instinctively it was still a threat. Once a day, it drifted to him as light fell from the shelters of the newcomers. They had blundered onto Eynar's land less than half a life ago and behaved strangely. They seemed to be always either angry or hungry, and behaved as if the land was all theirs.

The newcomers were unlike others in the forest. Voracious and loud, they seemed never to rest. Even great hunters like Eynar rested when well fed, but the newcomers seemed constantly to be making work for themselves. If they weren't killing to eat, they were cutting and killing for some other reason. Everything was their prey – plants and animals, big and small – and they didn't share with others in the forest.

Deer bit off pieces of tree, while beavers tipped some small trees whole. But the newcomers were like giant woodpeckers that cut right through. Even the biggest trees fell when they hit them, and it was never just one, but dozens and dozens. They often didn't stop until great swathes of the forest were flat, like after a mighty storm, or as the old folk stories told, when the sky above Tunguska in Siberia exploded, flattening trees for miles around.

Eynar thought the old stories sounded fantastical, but the elders insisted they were true. These newcomers didn't explode like brilliant, all-destroying stars crashing to earth, however. They just ate away at the world around them, relentlessly.

Eynar couldn't understand them. All their work

and industry didn't seem to make them happy. If anything they were like the mournful river spirits that conjure whirlpools by the rapids, sucking down anything unlucky enough to be caught in their downward pull, and from which there was no return.

The newcomers made Eynar uneasy, but mostly he could avoid them. By keeping to the denser, darker forest and moving at night, it was possible to go for weeks without ever seeing one. They were also so noisy walking and talking that Eynar and his family could hear them coming long before they came into sight, lie low or dodge around their path.

Yet as time passed, keeping away from them was getting harder. Their lairs encroached deeper and deeper into the woods and, whenever a new lair appeared, the woods around it changed. Trees disappeared, other different animals appeared, but these you couldn't hunt and, if you tried, some strange spell protected them. Eynar had seen his fellow hunters drop dead on the spot when they had tried to see if the meat of the new animals was good to eat. It led to all kinds of colourful suspicions among his kind, and questioning of the forest spirits.

Eynar was fed up. He wasn't used to worrying about anything much. He wanted back the world in which he could roam and feed his family without having to cower at unfamiliar smells or fear being struck dead by whatever spell protected the grunting, moaning, clucking new animal interlopers near his home. He wanted the forest back to its old order and determined to do something about it.

He vowed to visit the lair that had been built deepest into the wood and to try to make them understand the harm they were doing and that the forest was needed by others. When the sun was between its highpoint and disappearing underground, as it did when each day grew dark, he set off for the lair. Eynar never understood how the sun, when it re-emerged, was not covered in leaves, worms and twigs, because this always happened to him whenever he dug into the soil.

There was a gap in the flat logs piled at the entrance. Eynar was nervous because the creatures were so strange, but he was quietly confident too, as no other animal in the forest frightened him. Inside the lair the smell of burning was stronger. Suddenly he leapt back. There was a small trapped fire that somehow stayed in one place without drifting and climbing through the forest. How?

There were other smells too. Some were similar to ones you found among the trees, but much stronger. A big square log from which had flowers sprouting and blooming from its top reeked of lavender as if someone had buried his head in a bush of it, but this wasn't the time for lavender. Too many things were upside down. He smelled fish too, but this was miles from the river. How had they got here? A bird couldn't have dropped them because the lair had a roof, amazingly with no holes.

There was another smell too, a rare one, of something very, very old, but still alive. He'd smelled something similar only a few times before when a family member lived for many more seasons than usual. Now it was almost overpowering. Then he realized where it was coming from. That sound he thought was a mixture of the wind blowing through the lair's twigs and logs, and the leaf chatter in the trees above, was in fact the creature breathing. It seemed to be asleep. That was no good. How could he look into its eyes to let it know what needed to happen. A look from Eynar was usually enough for a creature of the forest to get the message.

With only slight trepidation, he went up to the sleeping form and nudged it. Nothing happened. He did it again, more firmly. It stirred. At the third nudge, its eyes opened. Then the most peculiar thing happened. This animal that slept deeply, and smelled so old, leapt and screeched like a night owl with murder on its mind. It moved fast and things flew like leaves and twigs in a storm. Eynar felt stung as if he had trodden and fallen into a thorn bush. It was like the creature was throwing the worst parts of the forest at him.

Eynar did what he would always do if another animal was foolish enough to try and take his place. With a few swift movements he made it go still, then cleaned it away. This was annoying because he really wanted the creature to take his message to the rest of its kind, but it also meant he would not need to hunt again for a while.

Then sleepy, he rested like any other wolf, preserving his energy. Then his acute hearing and sense of smell told him that another of the animals, not old-smelling this time, was approaching. He braced himself expecting the new one also to throw the forest at him, and realized that the strange loose skins of the old animal were still all over him. It had been tall, so he leapt up onto the odd bed of white moss to be at the same level, making eye-contact easier.

This one was young and female – he could tell by the smell again – with skins as red as the meadow poppies, the colour of fruit that could bring pleasure or death. The skins billowed around the animals head, enclosing its face like giant petals do to the part of the flower desired by bees. The young female stopped and threw nothing, but peered at Eynar, angling its head one way and then the other. On one arm were threaded twigs carrying the strange fruits these animals warmed and ate.

Eynar's look found its eyes and locked them in a gaze. He poured into the animal-poppy all the meanings he intended the creatures to understand. It made several low growls at him that he could not decipher. He spoke back in his own tongue, hoping it would understand. Did it, had it? He didn't know.

With his belly now full, he realized that if the hungry, angry animals did not leave the forest, he and his family could eat them instead. The other forest creatures would be pleased. With this thought in mind, contentedly he slid from the strange smelling lair back into the woods. Later, he saw the giant poppy head walking back to the other lairs and thought he would give her and her kind until the next bright moon to leave the forest before changing his family's diet.

19

The magical ladder

James Marriott

I am watching your mother talking with mine at the kitchen table. Her face is animated, her cheeks lined, her grey locks so neatly cut. The billow of silver hair above my mother's head is more disarrayed, but her eyes sparkle and she is smiling. Elsewhere in the room, unengaged in the conversation, there are others who come and go about their tasks. They are the help, the staff or whatever euphemism you choose use.

This is the home of my parents and I, in my fifties, still feel that familiar sense of unease, that slight sickness in the stomach, at being complicit in these hierarchies. This was the well in which I grew up. You threw a ladder down.

What was, and what is, that ladder? I am able to escape from this, to have the strength to visit it, but no longer feel entirely entombed, because of your faith in me, your love for me. All battered and bruised you help me climb up from the well.

The ladder is made by your difference from me. Your otherness and yet your desire to meet me as another. We come from such different worlds. According to the gravitational forces of class, we should never have met.

This fairy tale does not contain speaking animals or elves, but the bewitching escalator of fossil fuels and the enchanted elevator of social democracy.

Your grandmother was a servant in the household of a doctor from the age of fifteen. Your grandfather was a coal miner in a South Wales pit by fourteen. My grandmother was a daughter of an industrial plutocrat, the house and grounds were full of staff, from the chauffeur to the gardener, from the cook to the nanny. My grandfather was the son of a landed gentleman, his home was less grand but for sure there was a gardener and a cook, a nanny and a groom. We should never have met. Certainly not to fall in love and to live as equals.

Your great grandfather was killed, aged 35, by a rock fall in the Morfa Mawr. It was known as The Pit of Ghosts. The mines filled you forebears' lungs with black dust and shortened their lives, but there was wealth there, extracted through labour and struggle. And there was political muscle. The miners unions were the backbone of the beast that brought Labour to power in 1945.

With this victory, came the welfare state, which gave security to your class, and a government with the strength and will to tax the landholdings and portfolios of my class. Forty-six years later, we met, soon after stepping off the escalator of university. We've spent our lives together shouting in defence of the pillars of social democracy that held up the building in which we grew, and battling against the fossil fuels that are now drowning and burning our world.

I watch our mothers talking at the kitchen table. It is remarkable that they are here together. And you let down that magical ladder that enables me not to be dragged and sucked backwards in time.

With inspiration from Sharon van Etten

20

What the wind knows

Andrew Simms

Susurrate, they whisper, when I breathe between the trees. But your human word cannot convey the joy I feel to touch ten thousand leaves at once. Not to notice the world enough was one of your great mistakes.

We are the change makers, dune shapers, crop levellers. Trees bow before us and seas rise at our caress. We are everywhere and as restless as we make you feel.

Born of the slightest shift between my mother's warmth and father's chill, I learned from birth our old family tales. Now I carry a new story, the greatest yet to tell. You might call it our coming of age. Perhaps it is the end of yours. We don't know. That end is unwritten.

Unsettling, we blew through other's lives. Harsh grandfather Bora was the first to know. He played with the minds of men. Across the Adriatic, he took the happy and left them ill at ease, teasing chaos from the winter at Empires' end. He mocked as people fought to make new nations, blasting cold through Balkan borders as if they were not there. When the Great War left humans hungry for the energy of the sun, buried liquid and black beneath the earth, their red lines redrew maps where oil lay, scarring the ground with anger.

Bora then learned something, a century or more in the making, and passed it to my uncle, Levante. He was flippant and swaggering, heaved swells from the ocean, hot breath scorching across the troubled Straits of Gibraltar. Levante told Mistral, my distant, older and unknowable sister. Her cold, dry sigh haunted the unsuspecting on the hills of Southern France. She kept the secret knowledge and shared it with our dangerous cousin, Sirocco. People fear her when she lifts from the Saharan dunes like a circle dancer, spinning faster and faster.

Years ago, as a childish breeze she scared me too. Hurricane force and ferocious now, she whips Europe from Africa. Her brothers Simoom and Haboob suffocate the unwary with chaotic, dusty chronicles in their desert home. Nomads pass with respect, knowing not to listen.

Then, word of what our family knew caught the impatient jet stream. It spread as far as the Pacific

North West. Chinook, the snow-melter, first made the humans wonder. Had they finally learned our secret? Was it why they gave dull names like Mitch and Katrina, to those fierce, playful friends of ours who visit once a year, to still their fear?

We watched for two hundred years or more as, unwittingly, they fuelled our strength. Now I am nearly full grown, if I try to touch a leaf, it falls away in my fingers. I thought I knew myself, but sense I soon will take pleasure in other less innocent things, show tricks even my family cannot know, blow whole seas onto land, and those who stand in my path into the sea.

I wonder what they will call my new being? Unnamed, the final secret Bora learned was the new force within me, one that grows with the creeping warmth of the air. I fear the wind of change I am becoming. Can you imagine a name to make people think again?

21
And so it was...

Paul Allen

Once upon a time, not that long ago, Old Owl called a meeting. "My friends," he said. "How sad it is that our humanimal neighbours seem so very lonely. It breaks my heart to see them downcast. We must do something to help."

So every species dispatched envoys to observe their nearest humanimals and send their thoughts to a special gathering of the Grand Nature Council. It would work out what to do. Ideas poured in and Old Owl's advisors scoured them for any common theme.

The following week the Council assembled and, after several late nights, Old Owl stood up to speak.

"It seems," he said, "the humanimals no longer believe they are connected to nature or each other, or that nature itself is a living whole. Some even say they no longer believe that the Sun is conscious!"

Hearing Old Owl's words, the animals murmured in agreement. "Quite true, quite true, I heard that too," said several. "No wonder they feel so alone."

Then Young Raven spoke, with tears dropping from her eyes. "Something has gone wrong. For generations, humanimals knew the Sun was special". She went on to explain how Hindus saw the sun as a god called Surya, a red man with three eyes and four arms, who rode a chariot, pulled by a horse with seven heads. To the Norse, Freyr was the god of sunshine. He rode a boar named Gullinbursti, which carried him across the sky. For the Celts, Lugus was the sun god, a shimmering, brilliant warrior who helped win the war against the giants.

The animals listened in fascination. In ancient Greece the sun god Apollo, rode a chariot pulled across the sky by fiery horses. The ancient Egyptian's sun was a god called Ra, who was reborn each and every day. In Ghana, Benin, Togo, Alaska, Greenland, the Arctic, and almost everywhere else – people saw the sun as conscious.

Old Owl interrupted politely, supporting Raven, "I agree. Young humanimals have always drawn the sun with a face and a smile. Its consciousness was simply accepted. Everyone saw the Sun's light, heat, wind and waves as part of the life of every conscious creature on Earth. So what changed their minds?"

Young Raven spoke again. "As their science began to describe the universe, they recognized simple laws, to account for why a rock falls when you drop it, or predict how balls bounce off each other when you knock them together. But they were not yet clever enough to see the amazing complexity of very big or very small things. So when simple science rewrote the story of the sun, they were unable to see how very special it is. They thought it was just the chemical reactions of dead gasses. They tricked themselves into seeing consciousness as nothing more than their brains working like computers. Neither the Sun, then, nor the stars, nor the Earth nor indeed the Universe can be conscious – because they have nothing that looks like a brain."

By now, Young Raven was quite upset: "Ever since, they see almost everything as mechanical."

"Oh, no, no, no!" hooted Old Owl. "So when they see the beauty of a sunrise, all they see is a dead ball of gas. No wonder they're sad. What can we do?" Old Owl's question echoed around the Grand Nature Council: "Yes, what can we do, what can we do?"

Just then, Hedgehog raised her husky voice. "I have an idea" she said. "It's dangerous, but it might work. Someone must fly up, higher than high and talk to the Sun, will know what to do."

The animals quickly approved this plan. Old Owl volunteered but everyone knew his eyes were attuned to the dark night, and that the Sun would blind him. Then Young Raven said: "I will go, I can fly high."

"But you might burn," said Old Owl.

"But, how else can we dispel the humanimal sadness?" replied Young Raven. "I will do it when the frozen arctic winds are blowing to cool me."

So, later that month, as the icy arctic winds began to howl, Young Raven took flight. Long, long she flew, round and around in larger and larger circles, each one getting higher and higher. For three and a half exhausting days, she flew up, up towards the heavens, past the trees, beyond the highest mountains, above the wispy high clouds, until she thought the Sun might be close enough to hear her call.

But the Sun was too busy shining life down on the Earth to notice. So Young Raven began to sing her most beautiful song. The unusual sound drew the Sun's attention.

"Dear Sun," crowed the exhausted bird, "the humanimals think you are a dead ball of gas and have lost all wonder. What can I tell them?"

The Sun smiled upon Raven, and a hand-shaped solar flare shot across her path, lifting her into the Sun. Once inside, Raven's spirit joined with the Sun's and somehow, she immediately knew what the Sun was thinking. She saw those thoughts dance in ever-changing patterns of vibration. Understanding grew in her.

The energy of sunshine powers every living thing on earth. The Sun breathes in and out, and reverberates, like a gong, to over a million pitches, each bouncing back and forth through many layers inside, deep down right to a core. As particles move around, their electrical charges naturally create magnetic fields. A complicated system of cause and effect is created – churned by enormous heat from nuclear fusion at the core.

Vibrations, oscillations, perturbations, and harmonics from electromagnetic fields that ripple across my surface. Plasma near the Sun's poles rotates slower than at the equator, a bit like a swirling ball of porridge, causing the fields to twist and stretch. Every so often, they twist, twirl, lock up, and burst loose so intensely that they create auroras back on earth, disrupt radio signals or cause homing pigeons to lose their way.

Here was the Sun's consciousness and moods, just like the electromagnetic activity in brains of humanimals. "Once they see this," thought Raven, "they will feel more connected and less alone".

"Thank you dear Sun," said Raven, who by now was becoming singed around her feathers. "I will go down and tell them how to look at you more closely."

A quiet, uneasy feeling swept across the animal world. Everyone waited in nervous expectation for Raven to return. Like all of her kind, Raven's feathers had been snowy white, but the heat of the Sun turned them jet black, and so they would remain for all Ravens from then on.

Owl was the first to recognise her. "We celebrate your safe return. Did you discover how we can help the humanimals see the true wonder of the Sun?" he asked.

Raven thought then said: "We must tell a powerful story because their minds are too full of stuff."

Raven told what she learned at the heart of the Suns over and over until all knew it by heart.

Then, every animal on earth whispered the Sun's story to every humanimal they saw. Some said it so quietly, or while the humanimals were sleeping, that they didn't realize they were even listening. But, little by little, they started to look up and wonder.

New groups with curious names were formed like the Solar & Heliospheric Observatory Platform (S.H.O.P) and the Global Oscillation Network Group (G.O.N.G) – humanimals loved acronyms. They looked at big things and called it relativity, and they looked at very small things and called it quantum physics. They realized that their world and the universe was stranger than anyone imagined, and that how you looked at it changed what you saw. All these weird connections, and how reality was shaped by your point of view, was the consciousness the animals spoke of. From that day on, they began to leave their houses more, watched less TV, put their phones and computers to one side, spoke to each other more, walked in nature and looked upward, toward the Sun. They smiled and laughed more, felt more part of everything and seemed somehow more satisfied.

Not only did they now see the Sun differently, they discovered that they could use its energy to power the things they used in their homes, and needed less of the dirty fuel that filled their air with smoke and dirt.

"Well done, Raven!" said hedgehog dancing furiously in ever decreasing circles. Raven blushed and bowed, shining in her new jet-black plumage. Owl, Raven, Hedgehog and all the other animals, sang and danced in celebration till dawn, noon and then dusk on the following day, knowing that if the humanimals were happy, they too could live more in peace. Old Owl and Young Raven became best friends for life, even though one was big and fluffy and only came out at night, and the other was small, sleek and loved the sunshine.

22

The rise of the big bean counters

Molly Conisbee

Special Report: A Long Time Ago, in a Land Far Away...

Hipster promoters, food speculators and venture capitalists are helping companies develop indigenous food crops, to meet growing global demand for so-called 'super foods'. The resulting rise in food prices is creating protest and investment opportunities in equal measure. In a special Fairytale Economist report, Richard Whittington investigates...

I am sitting eating giant beans in a café in a newly gentrifying part of London, part of what the menu describes as a 'super-food' salad. The rise of super-foods, such as golden eggs®, bear porridge® and the latest must-have – giant beans® – has been a major growth area for the food business in recent years. Although super foods are nothing new – remember stepmother's 'sleepy-time apples'®, Alice's weight-loss tonic® or Lot's Himalayan pink salt®?- in the last decade, deregulation and speculation in food markets has ensured their production, patenting and distribution has become seriously big business for a number of emerging key players.

It is estimated that speculation in food commodities from hedge funds and banks, like Goldsacks and MidasTouch Bank has doubled in the last five years, pushing prices of key crops to their highest levels since the dish ran away with the spoon. High price levels can have little to do with the quantities of food available, but reflect the dominance of financial involvement in the food futures market, with shares of leading players up to 70 per cent in key commodities like magic pumpkins.

But food speculation is not just the financial arm of old school food industry, agri-business or giant producer and processor. Learning by taking the roots of ancient, heritage crop varieties, and patenting growing secrets passed from generation to generation, new players are emerging. Planted with seed funds from venture capital, powerful novel food-lifestyle brands are flourishing, replete with health claims, and cool new tastes and flavours.

You can sell even more if a celebrity chef can endorse your product. Who can forget the run on gingerbread after Hansel and Gretel's Granny Bake-Off? Welcome to the new food revolution.

Jack Stalker, my lunch companion, exemplifies the new kind of business-radical in the foodie field. Stalker carries the relaxed East London vibe of nu-folk beard, organic knitwear retro, more at home on his Brompton than in the boardroom. Stalker was himself brought up in a single-parent household, and his mother was a small-scale food producer.

"I know the food industry man and boy," he says. "Producers like my mother were wedded to certain ways of doing things. Her narrative ran like this: seasons, back to the land, no chems, third-party investment is a Generally Bad Thing. The old ways, if you will. Although I have the greatest of respect for her farming methods, she flatly refused the help of emerging technology to help her scale-up or improve her product. It was an epic imagination-fail on her part. The story of her brand became an irrelevant fable of yesteryear."

Stalker heads up The Saintly Bean®, a company which has in recent years specialized in developing carbon-neutral, giant bean varieties, with flavour, texture and heavily promoted anti-oxidants that are much prized in super-food circles. Stalker's latest giant bean variety has been so successful it has even overcome the resistance to genetic modification so often encountered in the food-conscious community, those most likely to buy into super-food brands. "It helps that The Saintly Bean® can actually help make you thin," he laughs. "Who can forget those bikini shots of Cinderella after the bean-detox?"

Stalker claims he has worked closely with the indigenous community whose giant beans The Saintly Bean® patented, to create what he describes as a "virtuous circle of environmentally-aware production, into a highly nutritious bean-product. The Saintly Bean's® vision is a super-conscious, highly ethical brand, which can reach out to the health-aware, the socially tuned-in, and those in pursuit of the hyper-tasty in equal measure. It's also a great source of vegan protein for those who want to tread lightly on the earth and their girth."

Stalker's company was founded with a loan from his mother's smallholding, financing which proved controversial in the early days of his enterprise when she accused him of fraudulently selling livestock to invest in a bean-technology plant. Mrs Stalker no longer comments on her son's business affairs, and has subsequently retired from farming to a tax haven in the Forest of Arden.

Stalker admits the early controversy around establishing the firm. "I needed capital. I was fortunate to have the seed funds from Mum, and then investment from a great bunch of venture futurologists, who gave me a lot of freedom to develop my product, as well as advice on marketing, brand, positioning, blitzscaling. It's been an amazing journey."

Producers hit back: Beans not so Saintly
But this has not been a journey without controversy. Food campaigners claim that enterprises like Stalker's, which are heavily backed by shadowy investors and equity firms, are destroying indigenous food supplies, through land-grabs and patenting ancient varieties of seeds and beans.

Stalker's giant beans have been a food staple for the Gulliver's Island people for generations. The tough growing conditions on their island mean it has taken years of careful selective breeding to develop the beans and other crops. Local community leaders argue they have been cheated out of rights to their crops by corporations such as The Saintly Bean®.

Jonathan Tall, a local food campaigner, says: "These crops took generations of painstaking care to develop. Our techniques and skills were passed orally, from generation to generation. In one fell swoop companies have bought the rights to patent our seeds, and pull the crop out from under our feet."

Has-Bean, a group established to campaign for the rights of the indigenous producers, argues that rights are systematically undermined through patents and increasing market speculation on food and other agricultural products. "We're in danger of creating a food system that is too big to fail – like banking. We all know what happened when the dragons swallowed all of the gold, and the taxpayer had to bail them out. The same deregulated principles are being applied to our food, with potentially devastating consequences," says Has-Bean's Head of Policy, Thomas Thumb.

Thumb continues: "Giant beans took generations to nurture and develop. Speculators like The Saintly Bean® have patented a plant that was never theirs to own. Our farmers now have to buy their beans from BeanCorp®, the major backer behind Stalker's enterprise. These seeds contain destructor genes, ensuring that new seeds and herbicides have to be bought annually. This is ruinous for small producers."

Stalker describes himself as "supremely relaxed" about the criticism from some indigenous producers. "Life moves on," he says. "The realities of a growing world population means we have to make more food out of land that is becoming less productive. The Gulliver's Island people have benefitted enormously from the investment ploughed into their infrastructure by The Saintly Bean®. The planet simply cannot sustain people living like little producers any more. We need bigger, better production systems, supported by values-based companies like mine. Life is not a fairytale."

The Saintly Bean® ploughs 1.5 per cent of annual profits into Island infrastructure, such as road, telecommunications and educational projects, including training for new harvesting and growing techniques. Unsubstantiated claims have been made by Has-Bean that the Island's President has received campaign funds from The Saintly Bean®, and her husband's business has also benefitted from investments held by BeanCorp®.

Big Beans are the future

The competing claims of community groups and business and developers are, of course, nothing new. Who can forget the protracted legal struggle between Lupus vs. Red Riding Hood Retirement Homes Development, or the widely publicised conditions revealed in the Stiltskin's clothing sweatshops last year?

At the time, we argued that the much-needed

investment and employment provided by such enterprises was a central platform of our Fairytale Economist agenda. Growth depends on supporting innovation and investment – without them the economy will wither and contract.

As Stalker notes: "Building a brand is telling a story. But sentimental tales about a golden age of making and growing are irrelevant in a world where people want quick results and quality products. I want to make wonderful things that consumers want, as efficiently as possible. My job is not to sort out whether the whole world can buy my beans or not. It's to keep my customers happy and well-fed."

The Saintly Bean® is making impressive returns for its investors. Enacting tighter regulations on investment in its production and futures, as campaigners call for, would discourage innovation, and stifle the green shoots of creatives like Stalker. Beans means less regulation, not more. So rising stars like Stalker stay sharp, a thousand bean stalks bloom, and new varieties and innovators continue to drive growth, profit, and widen consumer choice.

23

Impossible (the hamster)

Andrew Simms

Impossible was born on the day a bright new factory opened.

He had a strange name for a hamster. You'll soon see why.

Impossible was hungry.

Baby hamsters are.

In the first week, he drank all of his mother's milk, and doubled in size.

Baby hamsters do.

Still, he was hungry.

In the second week, he doubled again, and the third, fourth, fifth and sixth. It's a hamster habit.

Then *Impossible* should have slowed down.

Grown up hamsters do, like most living things.

But, from his wheel in the window, *Impossible* saw the new factory getting bigger and bigger. It was making quite a mess, but it also made some people very rich.

They bought bigger houses, bigger cars, and bigger televisions. They ate larger and larger plates of food. The people thought these things would make them happy. They didn't, but *Impossible* couldn't see that.

He thought: "Why should I stop growing if everything else is getting bigger?"

So he didn't.

First he ate his wheel and cage, and doubled in size again.

Then he started to eat his owner's house.

His owner shouted: "No! That's impossible."

It was, but he ate it anyway. And, doubled.

He found a park with a playground and started eating.

The children shouted: "No! That's impossible."

It was, but he ate it anyway. *Impossible* thought that the children's picnics tasted best which they dropped as they ran.

And he doubled again.

Then he saw a train leaving the town. It looked a
like a giant cardboard tube. Hamsters like tubes. So
Impossible started nibbling.

The passengers shouted: "No! That's impossible."

It was, but he ate it anyway. And doubled.

Impossible followed the train tracks to a city
where the buildings looked like food. One was like a
huge gherkin. He sniffed it.

The office workers inside shouted: "No!" But
guess what happened?

You might think steel and glass isn't tasty. But
remember all the biscuits and crisps people hide in
drawers, and the fruit they keep untouched in bowls
on tables.

Impossible ate the lot. And doubled.

Across the river, he saw a giant wheel. It was his
lucky day.

The tourists shouted: "'No!"

But *Impossible* climbed inside and started
running anyway.

Everywhere *Impossible* went, people said he was
too big to be a hamster. But *Impossible* couldn't
speak human. Hamsters don't.

As he ran, he thought of the factory that kept
growing, and the people who got bigger and bigger

things. "Getting larger must be good," he thought, in hamster language.

But now, even parks and playgrounds, trains and buildings were too small, even for a snack. On his first birthday he weighed 9 billion tonnes.

So, *Impossible* looked at Spain, a whole country. Everyone seemed to be cooking. It smelt good.

The Spanish people shouted:"'No! That really is impossible."

And of course it was, but that's why *Impossible* was his name. He ate it anyway... and doubled again.

Soon the world looked like the core of a mostly-eaten apple. *Impossible* clung on to the bit that was left. All the people – from the house, the park, the train, the gherkin, the wheel, and Spain, and everyone else who had nowhere left to go – clung on to *Impossible*.

No one knew what to do. They agreed it had been a silly idea to think that things could get bigger for ever and ever. If only they could have their old world back.

Just then, *Impossible* pulled a very funny face. After all that eating and eating, something sooner or later was going to happen. I know it sounds unlikely, but out came a world that was a bit smaller and a bit smellier than the one they had lost.

If you looked very closely, you could still see *Impossible*'s old wheel and cage inside his owner's house. There was the park and playground.

Of course it was. Whoever heard of a hamster digesting trees and swings and railings? And, there was the train and gherkin (it wasn't a real gherkin) and the country of Spain.

The bad smell soon went. People jumped and floated through space onto the new world and started to clean and tidy it up.

Impossible shrank back and felt much better. I think you would too. But he was still very big for a hamster. Everyone decided to be happy with fewer, smaller things on their new world. From then on, they were very, very careful when naming their hamsters.

Biographies of the authors

Paul Allen has lived and worked with renewable energy technologies for over 25 years. He trained as an electrical and electronic engineer and joined the Centre for Alternative Technology in 1988, developing a wide range of renewable energy systems including solar medical systems for use overseas. Paul has lead the ground-breaking Zero Carbon Britain research project for 10 years; liaising with Government, business, public sector and the arts. He has been a member of: the Wales Science Advisory Council (2010-14), the Climate Change Commission for Wales (2007-2015); the board of the International Forum for Sustainable Energy (2008-2013) and is a Fellow Royal Society of the Arts.

David Boyle is a writer and think-tanker, co-director of the New Weather Institute, and has been at the heart of the effort to develop co-production and introduce time banks to Britain as a critical element of public service reform. He was recently the government's independent reviewer on Barriers to Public Service Choice (2012-13). His book *Authenticity: Brands, Fakes, Spin and the Lust for Real Life* (2003) helped put the search for authenticity on the agenda as a social phenomenon. *The Tyranny of Numbers* (2001) predicted the backlash against the government's target culture. *Funny Money* (1999) launched the time banks movement in the UK. He also writes history books. Twitter: @davidboyle1958

Molly Conisbee is co-founder, with Ruth Potts, of anarchist baking, seditious pamphleteering and radical walking collective, bread, print and roses. After working in various policy and campaigning roles for, amongst others, the new economics foundation, IPPR and the Soil Association, Molly now researches the social history of death at the University of Bristol. She is co-author of *National Gardening Leave* and *Environmental Refugees* with Andrew Simms, and *Walk the Line* with David A. Wragg.

Jan Dean is a poet-in-schools whose work appears in over a hundred anthologies. Her latest book is The *Penguin in Lost Property* – written with Roger Stevens and published by Macmillan. She is a

National Poetry Day Ambassador for Forward Arts. Jan comes from the North West but now lives in Devon.

Carol Ann Duffy is Britain's first female, Scottish Poet Laureate in the role's 400 year history. Also a playwright, she is Professor of Contemporary Poetry at Manchester Metropolitan University. Her collections include *Standing Female Nude* (1985); *Selling Manhattan* (1987), winner of the Somerset Maugham Award; and *Rapture* (2005), winner of the T. S. Eliot Prize. Her writing combines tenderness and toughness, humour and lyricism, unconventional attitudes and conventional forms, has won her a very wide audience of readers and listeners.

Suki Ferguson is a writer, activist, and worker bee. She is co-author of the New Economy Organiser Network *Guide to Power & Privilege*, and lives in Hackney. She tweets about politics at @SukiKF

Hamish Fyfe is Professor of the Arts and Society at the University of South Wales. He is Director of the George Ewart Evans Centre for Storytelling which is the only research European research centre with storytelling as its focus. He is an Associate Editor of the Journal of Arts and Communities.

Rob Hopkins is the co-founder of Transition Town Totnes and of Transition Network. He is author of *The Transition Handbook: from oil dependence to local resilience,* and more recently of *The Power of Just Doing Stuff,* and *21 Stories of Transition.* He blogs at transitionnetwork.org, and tweets as @robintransition. He lectures and writes widely on Transition, and was one of the *Observer*'s '50 New Radicals'. He lives in Devon, grows food for his family, is the director of a social enterprise craft brewery, and of the ground-breaking Atmos Totnes community-led development project.

Kirsten Irving is one of the two editors behind award-winning poetry publisher, Sidekick Books. Her work has been shortlisted for the Bridport Prize, published by Salt and Happenstance, translated into Russian and Spanish, and thrown out of a helicopter. Kirsten works in London as a freelance copywriter, editor and voice actor. Her favourite fairytale is *Master of All Masters,* by Joseph Jacobs. www.kirstenirving.com

Rina Kuusipalo is a Master of Laws student at Stanford Law School, specialising in environmental law, with a background in human rights, climate change, and social and economic theory. She writes to make sense of things to herself and to dissect internally issues that she works on externally, yet often without extensive means for intuitive reflection. She believes law can also be immensely creative insofar as it pertains to the rules and norms underlying social organisation. Currently based in California, she grew up in Finland and previously lived in the UK and the US during her degrees at Harvard and Cambridge.

Lindsay Mackie is a partner in the New Weather Institute. She is a writer and campaigner who worked as a journalist on the *Guardian* and has run a number of campaigning charities. She is beginning to think that nature and the animal world are the most important things on our planet.

James Marriott is an artist and activist who works as part of Platform (www.platformlondon.org). Within this collective he has co-created projects ranging from opera to a micro-hydro plant and co-authored several books including *The Oil Road: journeys from the Caspian Sea to the City of London* (Verso 2012) with Milka Minio-Paluello. Platform's current work includes: Unravelling the Carbon Web focused on the human rights and environmental impacts of oil & gas corporations, in particular BP and Shell, and seeking to bring about their rapid closure.

Geoff Mead is a consultant, storyteller and the author of two books on the power of stories and storytelling: *Coming Home to Story: Storytelling Beyond Happily Ever After* (Vala, 2011) and *Telling the Story: The Heart and Soul of Successful Leadership* (Jossey-Bass, 2014). He is the founder of Narrative Leadership Associates, a consultancy focused on the use of storytelling for sustainable leadership. As an organizational consultant, keynote speaker and workshop leader, he has taken his work on narrative leadership onto the shopfloors and into the boardrooms of blue chip companies, charities, universities and government departments, for the past two decades (www.narrativeleadership.com). Geoff performs traditional stories at International Festivals and storytelling clubs and runs story-based workshops in the UK and as far afield as Spain, Canada and Japan.

Nick Robins works in London on sustainable finance. He has been head of SRI funds at Henderson Global Investors and head of HSBC's

Climate Change Centre. Currently he is co-director of UNEP's Inquiry into a Sustainable Financial System. He has published widely on sustainability issues and co-edited *Sustainable Investing: the Art of Long-term Performance.* He is also a historian and in 2006 published *The Corporation that Changed the World: How the East India Company Shaped the Modern Multinational.*

Nicky Saunter is a lover of fairy tales and an avid student of our modern condition. She has studied Chinese, Fine Monochrome Printing and Responsible Business Practice. Her working life encompasses the Economist Intelligence Unit, a US marketing company, a UK charity, a local food agency and three successful start-ups. She has spent far too much of her life writing reports and editing other people's work and is delighted to have the opportunity here to spread her wings a little.

Andrew Simms is a political economist, environmentalist and co-founder of the New Weather Institute. He is a research associate at the Centre for Global Political Economy, University of Sussex, and a fellow of the New Economics Foundation, where he was policy director for many years, running nef's work on climate change, energy and interdependence, and instigating their 'Great Transition' project. In work on local economies he coined the term 'clone towns' to describe the homogenization of high streets by chain stores. His books include *Tescopoly* and *Ecological Debt.* He co-authored *The New Economics, Eminent Corporations,* and the *Green New Deal*, devising the concept of 'ecological overshoot day' to illustrate when we begin living beyond our environmental means. Described by *New Scientist* magazine as "a master at joined-up progressive thinking", his latest book, *Cancel the Apocalypse: the New Path to Prosperity* is manifesto of new economic possibilities. tw: @andrewsimms_uk

Annes Stevens (cover designer) is an artist and illustrator with over eight years professional experience in the field of visual development. She has worked for industry-leading games studios EA Games and Lionhead and on prominent titles such as 'Harry Potter', 'Monopoly', 'Trivial Pursuits' and the award-winning 'Fable' franchise. She likes to develop new ideas and explore new styles, pushing visuals in a direction yet to be explored. Most recently, she has been working with Karrot Animation as art director on the new CBeebies animation series *Sarah & Duck.*

Fien Veldman was born and raised in Leeuwarden, The Netherlands. Her fiction has appeared in *De Correspondent, EXPOSED, de Fusie* and other publications. In 2015, she won the writing contest The Parliament of Things for the story included in this collection, and was awarded first prize in the Writer's Academy Short Story Contest. She holds a master's degree in Literary Studies from the University of Amsterdam and went to graduate school at McGill University, Montreal. She lives and works in Rotterdam.

Sarah Woods is a writer, performer, activist and facilitator whose work has been produced by companies including the RSC, Hampstead, Soho Theatre and the BBC, along with regional theatres and touring companies. She works with communities, campaigns, scientists and specialists. Current work includes *Bordered* for BBC Radio 4, about human rights and the migrant crisis, a new opera *Lazarus* for Birmingham Opera, and The Centre for Alternative Technology's *Zero Carbon: Making it Happen* report. Sarah is narrative artist with Cardboard Citizens, who make theatre with and for homeless people. She teaches playwriting at Manchester University and is a Wales Green Hero.

The New Weather Institute

We are a co-operative think-tank, focused on forecasting change and making the weather. We were created to accelerate the rapid transition to a fair economy that thrives within planetary boundaries. We bring together radical thinkers, scientists, economists, makers, artists and activists to find, design and advocate ways of working and living that are more humane, reasonable and effective.

Web: www.newweather.org
Twitter: @NewWeatherInst

Bread, Print & Roses

Founded by Ruth Potts and Molly Conisbee, bread, print & roses is a creative collective that explores new thinking and fresh approaches to living. We publish seditious pamphlets, lead and promote radical walks, host workshops in practical skills - from anarchist baking to community organising - and create spaces where people can come together to make change happen.

Web: www.breadprintandroses.org
Twitter: @printandroses

The Real Press
The Real Press is a small, independent publisher, specialising in history books with an edge, a description broad enough to include this one.

Web: www.therealpress.co.uk
Twitter: @therealpresspub